Acclaim for *War Fever*

"Ballard has an apocalyptic imagination, and his surreal portrayals of the future often display the shadows of last things so character-istic of science fiction . . . Narrowly focused but incisive, the stories transcend genre science fiction."
— Robert Taylor, *The Boston Globe*

"Clinical, dogmatic, relentlessly reifying and world-class imagina-tive, Ballard is really more a social critic than a storyteller . . . *War Fever* is an unusually tight, unified story collection."
— David Foster Wallace, *The Washington Post Book World*

"Outer space and inner space: in these 14 stories by J. G. Ballard, they seem almost the same . . . Ideas are Ballard's strength in this collection." — *Los Angeles Times Book Review*

"Each piece in *War Fever* is impeccably crafted, trenchantly witty, and strikes frighteningly close to home."
— Michael Upchurch, *San Francisco Review*

"J. G. Ballard is a master of extrapolation."
— Arthur Salm, *San Diego Tribune*

J. G. Ballard
War Fever

J. G. Ballard was born in Shanghai in 1930.
He is the author of more than twenty novels
and short-story collections. He lives in Shep-
perton, England.

By J. G. Ballard

J. G. Ballard

WAR FEVER

Farrar · Straus · Giroux

New York

Farrar, Straus and Giroux
19 Union Square West, New York 10003

Printed in the United States of America
First published in Great Britain by
William Collins Sons & Company Limited, 1990
First American edition published in 1991 by
Farrar, Straus and Giroux
First paperback edition, 1999

Library of Congress Cataloging-in-Publication Data
Ballard, J. G., 1930–
    War fever / J. G. Ballard.
        p.   cm.
    ISBN 0-374-52576-5 (pbk)
    I. Title.
PR6052.A46W37   1991
823´.914—dc20   90-27919

Author photograph © by Jerry Bauer

CONTENTS

WAR FEVER

War Fever

Ryan's dream of a cease-fire first came to him during the battle for the Beirut Hilton. At the time he was scarcely aware of the strange vision of a city at peace that had slipped uninvited into a corner of his head. All day the battle had moved from floor to floor of the ruined hotel, and Ryan had been too busy defending the barricade of restaurant tables in the mezzanine to think of anything else. By the end, when Arkady and Mikhail crept forward to silence the last Royalist sniper in the atrium, Ryan stood up and gave them covering fire, praying all the while for his sister Louisa, who was fighting in another unit of the Christian militia.

Then the firing ceased, and Captain Gomez signalled Ryan to make his way down the staircase to the reception area. Ryan watched the dust falling through the roof of the atrium fifteen floors above him. Illuminated by the sunlight, the pulverised cement formed a fleeting halo that cascaded towards the replica of a tropical island in the centre of the atrium. The miniature lagoon was filled with rubble, but a few tamarinds and exotic ferns survived among the furniture thrown down from the upper balconies. For a moment this derelict paradise was lit by the dust, like a stage set miraculously preserved in the debris of a bombed theatre. Ryan gazed at the fading halo, thinking that one day, perhaps, all the dust of Beirut would descend like the dove, and at last silence the guns.

But the halo served a more practical purpose. As Ryan followed Captain Gomez down the staircase he saw the two enemy militia men scrambling across the floor of the lagoon, their wet uniforms clearly visible against the chalky cement. Then he and Gomez were firing at the trapped soldiers, shredding the tamarinds into matchwood long after the two youths lay bloodily together in the

[1]

shallow water. Possibly they had been trying to surrender, but the newsreels of Royalist atrocities shown on television the previous evening put paid to that hope. Like the other young fighters, Ryan killed with a will.

Even so, as after all the battles in Beirut that summer, Ryan felt dazed and numbed when it was over. He could almost believe that he too had died. The other members of his platoon were propping the five bodies against the reception counter, where they could be photographed for the propaganda leaflets to be scattered over the Royalist strongholds in South Beirut. Trying to focus his eyes, Ryan stared at the roof of the atrium, where the last wisps of dust were still falling from the steel girders.

"Ryan! What is it?" Dr Edwards, the United Nations medical observer, took Ryan's arm and tried to steady him. "Did you see someone move up there?"

"No – there's nothing. I'm okay, doctor. There was a strange light . . ."

"Probably one of those new phosphorus shells the Royalists are using. A fiendish weapon, we're hoping to get them banned."

With a grimace of anger, Dr Edwards put on his battered UN helmet. Ryan was glad to see this brave, if slightly naïve man, in some ways more like an earnest young priest than a doctor, who spent as much time in the Beirut front line as any of the combatants. Dr Edwards could easily have returned to his comfortable New England practice, but he chose to devote himself to the men and women dying in a forgotten civil war half a world away. The seventeen-year-old Ryan had struck up a close friendship with Dr Edwards, and brought to him all his worries about his sister and aunt, and even his one-sided passion for Lieutenant Valentina, the strong-willed commander of the Christian guard-post at the telephone exchange.

Dr Edwards was always caring and sympathetic, and Ryan often exploited the physician's good nature, milking him for advance news of any shift in military alliances which the UN peace-keeping force had detected. Sometimes Ryan worried that Dr Edwards had spent too long in Beirut. He had become curiously addicted to the violence and death, as if tending the wounded and dying satisfied some defeatist strain in his character.

"Let's have a look at the poor devils." He led Ryan towards the soldiers propped against the reception counter, their weapons and personal letters arranged at their feet in a grim tableau. "With any luck, we'll find their next of kin."

Ryan pushed past Captain Gomez, who was muttering over his unco-operative camera. He knelt beside the youngest of the dead soldiers, a teenager with dark eyes and cherubic face, wearing the bulky camouflage jacket of the International Brigade.

"Angel . . . ? Angel Porrua . . . ?" Ryan touched the spongy cheeks of the fifteen-year-old Spaniard, with whom he often went swimming at the beaches of East Beirut. Only the previous Sunday they had rigged a makeshift sail on an abandoned dory and cruised half a mile up the coast before being turned back by the UN naval patrol. He realised that he had last seen Angel scrambling through the waterlogged debris of the artificial lagoon in the atrium. Perhaps he had recognised Ryan on the mezzanine staircase, and had been trying to surrender as he and Captain Gomez opened fire.

"Ryan?" Dr Edwards squatted beside him. "Do you know him?"

"Angel Porrua – but he's in the Brigade, doctor. They're on our side."

"Not any more." Clumsily, Dr Edwards pressed Ryan's shoulder in a gesture of comfort. "Last night they did a deal with the Royalists. I'm sorry – they've been guilty of real treachery."

"No, Angel was on our side . . ."

Ryan stood up and left the group of soldiers sharing a six-pack of beer. He stepped through the dust and rubble to the ornamental island in the centre of the atrium. The bullet-riddled tamarinds still clung to their rockery, and Ryan hoped that they would survive until the first of the winter rains fell through the roof. He looked back at the Royalist dead, sitting like neglected guests who had expired at the reception counter of this hotel, weapons beside them.

But what if the living were to lay down their weapons? Suppose that all over Beirut the rival soldiers were to place their rifles at their feet, along with their identity tags and the photographs of their sisters and sweethearts, each a modest shrine to a cease-fire?

*   *   *

[3]

A cease-fire? The phrase scarcely existed in Beirut's vocabulary, Ryan reflected, as he sat in the rear of Captain Gomez's jeep on the return to the Christian sector of the city. Around them stretched the endless vistas of shattered apartment houses and bombed-out office buildings. Many of the stores had been converted into strongpoints, their steel grilles plastered with slogans and posters, crude photographs of murdered women and children.

During the original civil war, thirty years earlier, more than half a million people had lived in Beirut. His own grandparents had been among them, some of the many Americans who had resigned their teaching posts at the schools and university to fight with the beleaguered Christian militia. From all over the world volunteers had been drawn to Beirut, mercenaries and idealists, religious fanatics and out-of-work bodyguards, who fought and died for one or another of the rival factions.

Deep in their bunkers below the rubble they even managed to marry and raise their families. Ryan's parents had been in their teens when they were murdered during the notorious Airport Massacre – in one of the worst of many atrocities, the Nationalist militia had executed their prisoners after promising them safe passage to Cyprus. Only the kindness of an Indian soldier in the UN force had saved Ryan's life – he had found the baby boy and his sister in an abandoned apartment building, and then tracked down their adolescent aunt.

However tragic, Beirut had been worth fighting for, a city with street markets, stores and restaurants. There were churches and mosques filled with real congregations, not heaps of roof-tiles under an open sky. Now the civilian population had gone, leaving a few thousand armed combatants and their families hiding in the ruins. They were fed and supplied by the UN peace-keeping force, who turned a blind eye to the clandestine shipments of arms and ammunition, for fear of favouring one or another side in the conflict.

So a futile war dragged on, so pointless that the world's news media had long since lost interest. Sometimes, in a ruined basement, Ryan came across a tattered copy of *Time* or *Paris Match*, filled with photographs of street-fighting and graphic reports on the agony of Beirut, a city then at the centre of the world's concern. Now no one cared, and only the hereditary militias fought on, grappling across their empires of rubble.

But there was nothing pointless about the bullets. As they passed the shell of the old pro-government radio station there was a single shot from the ground-floor window.

"Pull over, corporal! Get off the road!" Pistol in hand, Gomez wrenched the steering wheel from Arkady and slewed the jeep into the shelter of a derelict bus.

Kneeling beside the flattened rear tyres, Ryan watched the UN spotter plane circle overhead. He waited for Gomez to flush out the sniper, probably a Nationalist fanatic trying to avenge the death of a brother or cousin. The Nationalist militia were based at Beirut Airport, a wilderness of weed-grown concrete on which no plane had landed for ten years, and rarely ventured into the centre of the city.

If a cease-fire was ever to take hold it would be here, somewhere along the old Green Line that divided Beirut, in this no-man's-land between the main power bases – the Christians in north-east Beirut, the Nationalists and Fundamentalists in the south and west, the Royalists and Republicans in the south-east, with the International Brigade clinging to the fringes. But the real map of the city was endlessly redrawn by opportunist deals struck among the local commanders – a jeep bartered for a truckload of tomatoes, six rocket launchers for a video-recorder.

What ransom could buy a cease-fire?

"Wake up, Ryan! Let's move!" Gomez emerged from the radio station with his prisoner, a jittery twelve-year-old in a hand-me-down Nationalist uniform. Gomez held the boy by his matted hair, then flung him into the back of the jeep. "Ryan, keep an eye on this animal – he bites. We'll take him to interrogation."

"Right, captain. And if there's anything left we'll trade him for some new videos."

Hands bound, the boy knelt on the floor of the jeep, weeping openly from fear and rage. Jabbing him with his rifle stock, Ryan was surprised by his own emotions. For all his hopes of a cease-fire, he felt a reflex of real hate for this overgrown child. Hate was what kept the war going. Even Dr Edwards had been infected by it, and he wasn't alone. Ryan had seen the shining eyes of the UN observers as they photographed the latest atrocity victims, or debriefed the survivors of a cruel revenge attack, like prurient priests at confession. How could they put an end to the hate that was corrupting them all? Good God, he himself had begun to resent Angel Porrua for fighting with the Nationalists . . .

That evening Ryan rested on the balcony of Aunt Vera's apartment overlooking the harbour in East Beirut. He watched the riding lights of the UN patrol craft out at sea, and thought about his plans for a cease-fire. Trying to forget the day's fighting and Angel's death, he listened to Louisa chattering in the kitchen over the sounds of pop music broadcast by a local radio station.

The balcony was virtually Ryan's bedroom – he slept there in a hammock shielded from public view by the washing line and the plywood hutch he had built as a boy for his Dutch rabbit. Ryan could easily have moved to any one of the dozen empty apartments in the building, but he liked the intimacy of family life. The two rooms and kitchen were the only home he had ever known.

A young couple in an apartment across the street had recently adopted an orphan boy, and the sounds of his crying reminded Ryan that he at least was related by blood to the members of his family. In Beirut such blood ties were rare. Few of the young women soldiers ever conceived, and most children were war-orphans, though it puzzled Ryan where all these youngsters came from – somehow a secret family life survived in the basements and shantytowns on the outskirts of the city.

"That's the Rentons' new little son." His sister strolled onto the balcony, brushing out the waist-long hair that spent its days in a military bun. "It's a pity he cries a lot."

"At least he laughs more than he cries." An intriguing thought occurred to Ryan. "Tell me, Louisa – will Lieutenant Valentina and I have a child?"

"A child? Did you hear that, Aunty? So what does Valentina think?"

[6]

"I've no idea. As it happens, I've never spoken to her."

"Well, dear, I think you should ask her. She might lose something of her elegant composure."

"Only for a few seconds. She's very regal."

"It only takes a few seconds to conceive a child. Or is she so special that she won't even spare you those few seconds?"

"She is very special."

"Who's this?" Aunt Vera hung their combat jackets over the balcony, gazing at them with almost maternal pride. "Are you talking about me, Ryan, or your sister?"

"Someone far more special," Louisa rejoined. "His dream woman."

"You two are my dream women."

This was literally the truth. The possibility that anything might happen to them appalled Ryan. In the street below the balcony a night-commando patrol had lined up and were checking their equipment – machine-pistols, grenades, packs loaded with booby-traps and detonators. They would crawl into the darkness of West Beirut, each a killing machine out to murder some aunt or sister on a balcony.

A UN medical orderly moved down the line, issuing morphine ampoules. For all the lives they saved, Ryan sometimes resented the blue helmets. They nursed the wounded, gave cash and comfort to the bereaved, arranged foster-parents for the orphans, but they were too nervous of taking sides. They ringed the city, preventing anyone from entering or leaving, and in a sense controlled everything that went on in Beirut. They could virtually bring the war to a halt, but Dr Edwards repeatedly told Ryan that any attempt by the peace-keeping force to live up to its name would lead the world's powers to intervene militarily, for fear of destabilising the whole Middle East. So the fighting went on.

The night-commandos moved away, six soldiers on either side of the street, heading towards the intermittent clatter of gunfire.

"They're off now," Aunt Vera said. "Wish them luck."

"Why?" Ryan asked quietly. "What for?"

"What do you mean? You're always trying to shock us, Ryan. Don't you want them to come back?"

"Of course. But why leave in the first place? They could stay here."

"That's crazy talk." His sister placed a hand on Ryan's forehead, feeling for a temperature. "You had a hard time in the Hilton, Arkady told me. Remember what we're fighting for."

"I'm trying. Today I helped to kill Angel Porrua. What was he fighting for?"

"Are you serious? We're fighting for what we believe."

"But nobody believes anything! Think about it, Louisa. The Royalists don't want the King, the Nationalists secretly hope for partition, the Republicans want to do a deal with the Crown Prince of Monaco, the Christians are mostly atheists, and the Fundamentalists can't agree on a single fundamental. We're fighting and dying for nothing."

"So?" Louisa pointed with her brush to the UN observers by their post. "That just leaves them. What do they believe in?"

"Peace. World harmony. An end to fighting everywhere."

"Then maybe you should join them."

"Yes . . ." Ryan pushed aside his combat jacket and stared through the balcony railings. Each of the blue helmets was a pale lantern in the dusk. "Maybe we should all join the UN. Yes, Louisa, everyone should wear the blue helmet."

And so a dream was born.

During the next days Ryan began to explore this simple but revolutionary idea. Though gripped by the notion, he knew that it was difficult to put into practice. His sister was sceptical, and the fellow members of his platoon were merely baffled by the concept.

"I see what you're getting at," Arkady admitted as they shared a cigarette in the Green Line command bunker. "But if everyone joins the UN who will be left to do the fighting?"

"Arkady, that's the whole point . . ." Ryan was tempted to give up. "Just think of it. Everything will be neat and clean again. There'll be no more patrols, no parades or weapons drills. We'll lie around in the McDonald's eating hamburgers; there'll be discos every night. People will be walking around the streets, going into stores, sitting in cafés . . ."

"That sounds really weird," Arkady commented.

"It isn't weird. Life will start again. It's how it used to be, like it is now in other places around the world."

"Where?"

"Well . . ." This was a difficult one. Like the other fighters in Beirut, Ryan knew next to nothing about the outside world. No newspapers came in, and foreign TV and radio broadcasts were jammed by the signals teams of the rival groups to prevent any foreign connivance in a military coup. Ryan had spent a few years in the UN school in East Beirut, but his main source of information about the larger world was the forty-year-old news magazines that he found in abandoned buildings. These presented a picture of a world at strife, of bitter fighting in Viet Nam, Angola and Iran. Presumably these vast conflicts, greater versions of the fighting in Beirut, were still going on.

Perhaps the whole world should wear the blue helmet? This thought excited Ryan. If he could bring about a cease-fire in Beirut the peace movement might spread to Asia and Africa, everyone would lay down their arms . . .

Despite numerous rebuffs Ryan pressed on, arguing his case with any soldiers he met. Always there was an unvoiced interest, but one obstacle was the constant barrage of propaganda – the atrocity posters, the TV newsreels of vandalised churches that played on an ever-ready sense of religious outrage, and a medley of racial and anti-monarchist slanders.

To break this propaganda stranglehold was far beyond Ryan's powers, but by chance he found an unexpectedly potent weapon – humour.

While on duty with a shore patrol by the harbour, Ryan was describing his dream of a better Beirut as his unit passed the UN command post. The observers had left their helmets on the open-air map table, and without thinking Ryan pulled off his khaki forage cap and lowered the blue steel bowl over his head.

"Hey, look at Ryan!" Arkady shouted. There was some good-humoured scuffling until Mikhail and Nazar pulled them apart. "No more wrestling now, we have our own peace-keeping force!"

Friendly cat-calls greeted Ryan as he paraded up and down in the helmet, but then everyone fell silent. The helmet had a calming effect, Ryan noticed, both on himself and his fellow-soldiers. On an impulse he set off along the beach towards the Fundamentalist sentry-post 500 yards away.

"Ryan – look out!" Mikhail ran after him, but stopped as Captain Gomez rode up in his jeep to the harbour wall. Together they watched as Ryan strode along the shore, ignoring the sniper-infested office buildings. He was halfway to the sentry-post when a Fundamentalist sergeant climbed onto the roof, waving a temporary safe-passage. Too cautious to risk his charmed life, Ryan saluted and turned back.

When he rejoined his platoon everyone gazed at him with renewed respect. Arkady and Nazar were wearing blue helmets, sheepishly ignoring Captain Gomez as he stepped in an ominous way from his jeep. Then Dr Edwards emerged from the UN post, restraining Gomez.

"I'll take care of this, captain. The UN won't press charges. I know Ryan wasn't playing the fool."

Explaining his project to Dr Edwards was far easier than Ryan had hoped. They sat together in the observation post, as Dr Edwards encouraged him to outline his plan.

"It's a remarkable idea, Ryan." Clearly gripped by its possibilities, Dr Edwards seemed almost lightheaded. "I won't say it's going to work, but it deserves a try."

"The main object is the cease-fire," Ryan stressed. "Joining the UN force is just a means to that end."

"Of course. But do you think they'll wear the blue helmet?"

"A few will, but that's all we need. Little by little, more people will join up. Everyone is sick of fighting, doctor, but there's nothing else here."

"I know that, Ryan. God knows it's a desperate place." Dr Edwards reached across the table and held Ryan's wrists, trying to lend him something of his own strength. "I'll have to take this up with the UN Secretariat in Damascus, so it's vital to get it right. Let's think of it as a volunteer UN force."

[10]

"Exactly. We'll volunteer to wear the blue helmet. That way we don't have to change sides or betray our own people. Eventually, everyone will be in the volunteer force . . ."

". . . and the fighting will just fade away. It's a great idea, it's only strange that no one has ever thought of it before." Dr Edwards was watching Ryan keenly. "Did anyone help you? One of the wounded ex-officers, perhaps?"

"There wasn't anyone, doctor. It just came to me, out of all the death . . ."

Dr Edwards left Beirut for a week, consulting his superiors in Damascus, but in that time events moved more quickly than Ryan had believed possible. Everywhere the militia fighters were sporting the blue helmet. This began as a joke confined to the Christian forces, in part an irreverent gesture at the UN observers. Then, while patrolling the Green Line, Ryan spotted the driver of a Royalist jeep wearing a blue beret. Soon the more carefree spirits, the pranksters in every unit, wore the helmet or beret like a cockade.

"Ryan, look at this." Captain Gomez called him to the command post in the lobby of the TV station. "You've got a lot to answer for . . ."

Across the street, near a burnt-out Mercedes, a Royalist guerrilla in a blue beret had set up a canvas chair and card table. He sat back, feet on the table, leisurely taking the sun.

"The nerve of it . . ." Gomez raised Ryan's rifle and trained it at the soldier. He whistled to himself, and then handed the weapon back to Ryan. "He's lucky, we're over-exposed here. I'll give him his suntan . . ."

This was a breakthrough, and not the last. Clearly there was a deep undercurrent of fatigue. By the day of Dr Edwards' return, Ryan estimated that one in ten of the militia fighters was wearing the blue helmet or beret. Fire-fights still shook the night sky, but the bursts of gunfire seemed more isolated.

"Ryan, it's scarcely credible," Dr Edwards told him when they met at the UN post near the harbour. He pointed to the map marked with a maze of boundary lines and fortified positions. "Today there

[11]

hasn't been a single major incident along the Green Line. North of the airport there's even a de facto cease-fire between the Fundamentalists and the Nationalists."

Ryan was staring at the sea, where a party of Christian soldiers were swimming from a diving-raft. The UN guard-ships were close inshore, no longer worried about drawing fire. Without meaning to dwell on the past, Ryan said: "Angel and I went sailing there."

"And you'll go sailing again, with Nazar and Arkady." Dr Edwards seized his shoulders. "Ryan, you've brought off a miracle!"

"Well . . ." Ryan felt unsure of his own emotions, like someone who has just won the largest prize in a lottery. The UN truck parked in the sun was loaded with crates of blue uniforms, berets and helmets. Permission had been granted for the formation of a volunteer UN force recruited from the militias. The volunteers would serve in their own platoons, but be unarmed and take no part in any fighting, unless their lives were threatened. The prospect of a permanent peace was at last in sight.

Only six weeks after Ryan had first donned the blue helmet, an unbroken cease-fire reigned over Beirut. Everywhere the guns were silent. Sitting beside Captain Gomez as they toured the city by jeep, Ryan marvelled at the transformation. Unarmed soldiers lounged on the steps of the Hilton, groups of once-bitter enemies fraternised on the terrace of the Parliament building. Shutters were opening on the stores along the Green Line, and there was even a modest street market in the hallway of the Post Office. Children had emerged from their basement hideaways and played among the burnt-out cars. Many of the women guerrillas had exchanged their combat fatigues for bright print dresses, a first taste of the glamour and chic for which the city had once been renowned.

Even Lieutenant Valentina now stalked about in a black leather skirt and vivid lipstick jacket, blue beret worn rakishly over an elegant chignon.

As they passed her command post Captain Gomez stopped the jeep. He doffed his blue helmet in a gesture of respect. "My God! Isn't that the last word, Ryan?"

"It certainly is, captain," Ryan agreed devoutly. "How do I even dare approach her?"

"What?" Gomez followed Ryan's awestruck gaze. "Not Lieutenant Valentina – she'll eat you for breakfast. I'm talking about the soccer match this afternoon."

He pointed to the large poster recently pasted over the cracked windows of the nearby Holiday Inn. A soccer match between the Republican and Nationalist teams would take place at three o'clock in the stadium, the first game in the newly formed Beirut Football League.

"'Tomorrow – Christians versus Fundamentalists. Referee: Colonel Mugabe of the International Brigade.' That should be high-scoring . . ." Blue helmet in hand, Gomez climbed from the jeep and strolled over to the poster.

Ryan, meanwhile, was staring at Lieutenant Valentina. Out of uniform she seemed even more magnificent, her Uzi machine-pistol slung over her shoulder like a fashion accessory. Taking his courage in both hands, Ryan stepped into the street and walked towards her. She could eat him for breakfast, of course, and happily lunch and supper as well . . .

The lieutenant turned her imperious eyes in his direction, already resigned to the attentions of this shy young man. But before Ryan could speak, an immense explosion erupted from the street behind the TV station. The impact shook the ground and drummed against the pockmarked buildings. Fragments of masonry cascaded into the road as a cloud of smoke seethed into the sky, whipped upwards by the flames that rose from the detonation point somewhere to the south-west of the Christian enclave.

A six-foot scimitar of plate glass fell from the window of the Holiday Inn, slicing through the football poster, and shattered around Gomez's feet. As he ran to the jeep, shouting at Ryan, there was a second explosion from the Fundamentalist sector of West Beirut. Signal flares were falling in clusters over the city, and the first rounds of gunfire competed with the whine of klaxons and the loudspeakers broadcasting a call to arms.

Ryan stumbled to his feet, brushing the dust from his combat jacket. Lieutenant Valentina had vanished into the strongpoint, where her men were already loading the machine-gun in the barbette.

"Captain Gomez . . . The bomb? What set it off?"

"Treachery, Ryan – the Royalists must have done a deal with the Nats." He pulled Ryan into the jeep, cuffing him over the head. "All this talk of peace. The oldest trap in the world, and we walked straight into it . . ."

More than treachery, however, had taken place. Armed militia men filled the streets, taking up their positions in the blockhouses and strongpoints. Everyone was shouting at once, voices drowned by the gunfire that came from all directions. Powerful bombs had been cunningly planted to cause maximum confusion, and the nervous younger soldiers were firing into the air to keep up their courage. Signal flares were falling over the city in calculated but mysterious patterns. Everywhere blue helmets and berets were lying discarded in the gutter.

When Ryan reached his aunt's apartment he found Dr Edwards and two UN guards waiting for him.

"Ryan, it's too late. I'm sorry."

Ryan tried to step past to the staircase, but Dr Edwards held his arms. Looking up at this anxious and exhausted man, Ryan realised that apart from the UN observers he was probably the only one in Beirut still wearing the blue helmet.

"Dr Edwards, I have to look after Louisa and my aunt. They're upstairs."

"No, Ryan. They're not here any longer. I'm afraid they've gone."

"Where? My God, I told them to stay here!"

"They've been taken as hostages. There was a commando raid timed for the first explosion. Before we realised it, they were in and out."

"Who?" Confused and frightened, Ryan stared wildly at the street, where armed men were forming into their platoons. "Was it the Royalists, or the Nats?"

"We don't know. It's tragic, already there have been some foul atrocities. But they won't harm Louisa or your aunt. They know who you are."

"They took them because of *me* . . ." Ryan lifted the helmet from his head. He stared at the blue bowl, which he had carefully polished, trying to make it the brightest in Beirut.

"What do you plan to do, Ryan?" Dr Edwards took the helmet from his hands, a stage prop no longer needed after the last curtain. "It's your decision. If you want to go back to your unit, we'll understand."

Behind Dr Edwards one of the observers held Ryan's rifle and webbing. The sight of the weapon and its steel-tipped bullets brought back Ryan's old anger, that vague hatred that had kept them all going for so many years. He needed to go out into the streets, track down the kidnappers, revenge himself on those who had threatened his aunt and Louisa.

"Well, Ryan . . ." Dr Edwards was watching him in a curiously distant way, as if Ryan was a laboratory rat at a significant junction in a maze. "Are you going to fight?"

"Yes, I'll fight . . ." Ryan placed the blue helmet firmly on his head. "But not for war. I'll work for another cease-fire, doctor."

It was then that he found himself facing the raised barrel of his own rifle. An expressionless Dr Edwards took his wrists, but it was some minutes before Ryan realised that he had been handcuffed and placed under arrest.

For an hour they drove south-east through the suburbs of Beirut, past the derelict factories and shantytowns, stopping at the UN checkpoints along the route. From his seat in the back of the armoured van, Ryan could see the ruined skyline of the city. Funnels of smoke leaned across the sky, but the sound of gunfire had faded. Once they stopped to stretch their legs, but Dr Edwards declined to talk to him. Ryan assumed that the physician suspected him of being involved with the conspirators who had broken the cease-fire. Perhaps Dr Edwards imagined that the whole notion of cease-fire had been a devious scheme in which Ryan had exploited his contacts among the young . . . ?

They passed through the second of the perimeter fences that enclosed the city, and soon after approached the gates of a military camp built beside a deserted sanatorium. A line of olive-green tents covered the spacious grounds. Arrays of radio antennae and television dishes rose from the roof of the sanatorium, all facing north-west towards Beirut.

The van stopped at the largest of the tents, which appeared to house a hospital for wounded guerrillas. But within the cool green interior there was no sign of patients. Instead they were walking through a substantial arsenal. Rows of trestle tables were loaded with carbines and machine-guns, boxes of grenades and mortar bombs. A UN sergeant moved among this mountain of weaponry, marking items on a list like the owner of a gun store checking the day's orders.

Beyond the arsenal was an open area that resembled the newsroom of a television station. A busy staff of UN observers stood beneath a wall map of Beirut, moving dozens of coloured tapes and stars. These marked the latest positions in the battle for the city being screened on the TV monitors beside the map.

"You can leave us, corporal. I'll be in charge of him now." Dr Edwards took the rifle and webbing from the UN guard, and beckoned Ryan into a canvas-walled office at the end of the tent. Plastic windows provided a clear view into an adjacent room, where two women clerks were rolling copies of a large poster through a printing press. The blown-up photograph of a Republican atrocity, it showed a group of murdered women who had been executed in a basement garage.

Staring at this gruesome image, Ryan guessed why Dr Edwards still avoided his eyes.

"Dr Edwards, I didn't know about the bomb this morning, or the surprise attack. Believe me –"

"I believe you, Ryan. Everything's fine, so try to relax." He spoke curtly, as if addressing a difficult patient. He laid the rifle on his desk, and released the handcuffs from Ryan's wrists. "You're out of Beirut for good now. As far as you're concerned, the cease-fire is permanent."

"But . . . what about my aunt and sister?"

"They've come to no harm. In fact, at this very moment

[16]

they're being held at the UN post near the Football Stadium."

"Thank God. I don't know what went wrong. Everyone wanted the cease-fire . . ." Ryan turned from the atrocity posters spilling endlessly through the slim hands of the UN clerks. Pinned to the canvas wall behind Dr Edwards were scores of photographs of young men and women in their combat fatigues, caught unawares near the UN observation posts. In pride of place was a large photograph of Ryan himself. Assembled together, they resembled the inmates of a mental institution.

Two orderlies passed the doorway of the office, wheeling a trolley loaded with assault rifles.

"These weapons, doctor? Are they confiscated?"

"No – as it happens, they're factory-new. They're on their way to the battlefield."

"So there's more fighting going on outside Beirut . . ." This news was enough to make Ryan despair. "The whole world's at war."

"No, Ryan. The whole world is at peace. Except for Beirut – that's where the weapons are going. They'll be smuggled into the city inside a cargo of oranges."

"Why? That's mad, doctor! The militias will get them!"

"That's the point, Ryan. We want them to have the weapons. And we want them to keep on fighting."

Ryan began to protest, but Dr Edwards showed him firmly to the chair beside the desk.

"Don't worry, Ryan, I'll explain it all to you. Tell me first, though – have you ever heard of a disease called smallpox?"

"It was some sort of terrible fever. It doesn't exist any more."

"That's true – almost. Fifty years ago the World Health Organisation launched a huge campaign to eliminate smallpox, one of the worst diseases mankind has ever known, a real killer that destroyed tens of millions of lives. There was a global programme of vaccination, involving doctors and governments in every country. Together they finally wiped it from the face of the earth."

"I'm glad, doctor – if only we could do the same for war."

"Well, in a real sense we have, Ryan – almost. In the case of small-pox, people can now travel freely all over the world. The virus does survive in ancient graves and cemeteries, but if by some freak chance the disease appears again there are supplies of vaccine to protect people and stamp it out."

Dr Edwards detached the magazine from Ryan's rifle and weighed it in his hands, showing an easy familiarity with the weapon that Ryan had never seen before. Aware of Ryan's surprise, he smiled wanly at the young man, like a headmaster still attached to a delinquent pupil.

"Left to itself, the smallpox virus is constantly mutating. We have to make sure that our supplies of vaccine are up-to-date. So WHO was careful never to completely abolish the disease. It deliberately allowed smallpox to flourish in a remote corner of a Third World country, so that it could keep an eye on how the virus was evolving. Sadly, a few people went on dying, and are still dying to this day. But it's worth it for the rest of the world. That way we'll always be ready if there's an outbreak of the disease."

Ryan stared through the plastic windows at the wall map of Beirut and the TV monitors with their scenes of smoke and gunfire. The Hilton was burning again.

"And Beirut, doctor? Here you're keeping an eye on another virus?"

"That's right, Ryan. The virus of war. Or, if you like, the martial spirit. Not a physical virus, but a psychological one even more dangerous than smallpox. The world is at peace, Ryan. There hasn't been a war anywhere for thirty years – there are no armies or air forces, and all disputes are settled by negotiation and compromise, as they should be. No one would dream of going to war, any more than a sane mother would shoot her own children if she was cross with them. But we have to protect ourselves against the possibility of a mad strain emerging, against the chance that another Hitler or Pol Pot might appear."

"And you can do all that here?" Ryan scoffed. "In Beirut?"

"We think so. We have to see what makes people fight, what makes them hate each other enough to want to kill. We need to know how we can manipulate their emotions, how we can twist the news and trigger off their aggressive drives, how we can play on their religious feelings or political ideals. We even need to know how strong the desire for peace is."

[18]

"Strong enough. It can be strong, doctor."

"In your case, yes. You defeated us, Ryan. That's why we've pulled you out." Dr Edwards spoke without regret, as if he envied Ryan his dogged dream. "It's a credit to you, but the experiment must go on, so that we can understand this terrifying virus."

"And the bombs this morning? The surprise attack?"

"We set off the bombs, though we were careful that no one was hurt. We supply all the weapons, and always have. We print up the propaganda material, we fake the atrocity photographs, so that the rival groups betray each other and change sides. It sounds like a grim version of musical chairs, and in a way it is."

"But all these years, doctor . . ." Ryan was thinking of his old comrades-in-arms who had died beside him in the dusty rubble. Some had given their lives to help wounded friends. "Angel and Moshe, Aziz . . . hundreds of people dying!"

"Just as hundreds are still dying of smallpox. But thousands of millions are living – in peace. It's worth it, Ryan; we've learned so much since the UN rebuilt Beirut thirty years ago."

"They planned it all – the Hilton, the TV station, the McDonald's . . . ?"

"Everything, even the McDonald's. The UN architects designed it as a typical world city – a Hilton, a Holiday Inn, a sports stadium, shopping malls. They brought in orphaned teenagers from all over the world, from every race and nationality. To begin with we had to prime the pump – the NCOs and officers were all UN observers fighting in disguise. But once the engine began to turn, it ran with very little help."

"Just a few atrocity photographs . . ." Ryan stood up and began to put on his webbing. Whatever he thought of Dr Edwards, the reality of the civil war remained, the only logic that he recognised. "Doctor, I have to go back to Beirut."

"It's too late, Ryan. If we let you return, you'd endanger the whole experiment."

"No one will believe me, doctor. Anyway, I must find my sister and Aunt Vera."

"She isn't your sister, Ryan. Not your real sister. And Vera isn't your real aunt. They don't know, of course. They think you're

[19]

all from the same family. Louisa was the daughter of two French explorers from Marseilles who died in Antarctica. Vera was a foundling brought up by nuns in Montevideo."

"And what about . . . ?"

"You, Ryan? Your parents lived in Halifax, Nova Scotia. You were three months old when they were killed in a car crash. Sadly, there are some deaths we can't yet stop . . ."

Dr Edwards was frowning at the wall map of Beirut visible through the plastic window. A signals sergeant worked frantically at the huge display, pinning on clusters of incident flags. Everyone had gathered around the monitor screens. An officer waved urgently to Dr Edwards, who stood up and left the office. Ryan stared at his hands while the two men conferred, and he scarcely heard the physician when he returned and searched for his helmet and side-arm.

"They've shot down the spotter plane. I'll have to leave you, Ryan – the fighting's getting out of control. The Royalists have overrun the Football Stadium and taken the UN post."

"The Stadium?" Ryan was on his feet, his rifle the only security he had known since leaving the city. "My sister and aunt are there! I'll come with you, doctor."

"Ryan . . . everything's starting to fall apart; we may have lit one fuse too many. Some of the militia units are shooting openly at the UN observers." Dr Edwards stopped Ryan at the door. "I know you're concerned for them, you've lived with them all your life. But they're not –"

Ryan pushed him away. "Doctor, they *are* my aunt and sister."

It was three hours later when they reached the Football Stadium. As the convoy of UN vehicles edged its way into the city, Ryan gazed at the pall of smoke that covered the ruined skyline. The dark mantle extended far out to sea, lit by the flashes of high explosives as rival demolition squads moved through the streets. He sat behind Dr Edwards in the second of the armoured vans, but they could scarcely hear themselves talk above the sounds of rocket and machine-gun fire.

By this stage Ryan knew that he and Dr Edwards had little to say to each other. Ryan was thinking only of the hostages in the overrun UN post. His discovery that the civil war in Beirut was an elaborate experiment belonged to a numb area outside his mind, an emotional black hole from which no light or meaning could escape.

At last they stopped near the UN post at the harbour in East Beirut. Dr Edwards sprinted to the radio shack, and Ryan unstrapped his blue helmet. In a sense he shared the blame for this uncontrolled explosion of violence. The rats in the war laboratory had been happy pulling a familiar set of levers – the triggers of their rifles and mortars – and being fed their daily pellets of hate. Ryan's dazed dream of peace, like an untested narcotic, had disoriented them and laid them open to a frenzy of hyperactive rage . . .

"Ryan, good news!" Dr Edwards hammered on the windscreen, ordering the driver to move on. "Christian commandos have retaken the Stadium!"

"And my sister? And Aunt Vera?"

"I don't know. Hope for the best. At least the UN is back in action. With luck, everything will return to normal."

Later, as he stood in the sombre storeroom below the concrete grandstand, Ryan reflected on the ominous word that Dr Edwards had used. Normal . . . ? The lights of the photographers' flashes illuminated the bodies of the twenty hostages laid against the rear wall. Louisa and Aunt Vera rested between two UN observers, all executed by the Royalists before their retreat. The stepped concrete roof was splashed with blood, as if an invisible audience watching the destruction of the city from the comfort of the grandstand had begun to bleed into its seats. Yes, Ryan vowed, the world would bleed . . .

The photographers withdrew, leaving Ryan alone with Louisa and his aunt. Soon their images would be scattered across the ruined streets, pasted to the blockhouse walls.

"Ryan, we ought to leave before there's a counterattack." Dr Edwards stepped through the pale light. "I'm sorry about them – whatever else, they *were* your sister and aunt."

"Yes, they were . . ."

[21]

"And at least they helped to prove something. We need to see how far human beings can be pushed." Dr Edwards gestured helplessly at the bodies. "Sadly, all the way."

Ryan took off his blue helmet and placed it at his feet. He snapped back the rifle bolt and drove a steel-tipped round into the breech. He was only sorry that Dr Edwards would lie beside Louisa and his aunt. Outside there was a momentary lull in the fighting, but it would resume. Within a few months he would unite the militias into a single force. Already Ryan was thinking of the world beyond Beirut, of that far larger laboratory waiting to be tested, with its millions of docile specimens unprepared for the most virulent virus of them all.

"Not all the way, doctor." He levelled the rifle at the physician's head. "All the way is the whole human race."

(1989)

The Secret History of World War 3

Now that World War 3 has safely ended, I feel free to comment on two remarkable aspects of the whole terrifying affair. The first is that this long-dreaded nuclear confrontation, which was widely expected to erase all life from our planet, in fact lasted barely four minutes. This will surprise many of those reading the present document, but World War 3 took place on 27 January 1995, between 6:47 and 6:51 p.m. Eastern Standard Time. The entire duration of hostilities, from President Reagan's formal declaration of war, to the launch of five sea-based nuclear missiles (three American and two Russian), to the first peace-feelers and the armistice agreed by the President and Mr Gorbachev, lasted no more than 245 seconds. World War 3 was over almost before anyone realised that it had begun.

The other extraordinary feature of World War 3 is that I am virtually the only person to know that it ever occurred. It may seem strange that a suburban paediatrician living in Arlington, a few miles west of Washington, D.C., should alone be aware of this unique historical event. After all, the news of every downward step in the deepening political crisis, the ailing President's declaration of war and the following nuclear exchange, was openly broadcast on nationwide television. World War 3 was not a secret, but people's minds were addressed to more important matters. In their obsessive concern for the health of their political leadership, they were miraculously able to ignore a far greater threat to their own well-being.

Of course, strictly speaking, I was not the only person to have witnessed World War 3. A small number of senior military personnel in the NATO and Warsaw Pact high commands, as well as President

Reagan, Mr Gorbachev and their aides, and the submarine officers who decrypted the nuclear launch codes and sent the missiles on their way (into unpopulated areas of Alaska and eastern Siberia), were well aware that war had been declared, and a cease-fire agreed four minutes later. But I have yet to meet a member of the ordinary public who has heard of World War 3. Whenever I refer to the war, people stare at me with incredulity. Several parents have withdrawn their children from the paediatric clinic, obviously concerned for my mental stability. Only yesterday one mother to whom I casually mentioned the war later telephoned my wife to express her anxieties. But Susan, like everyone else, has forgotten the war, even though I have played video-recordings to her of the ABC, NBC and CNN newscasts on 27 January which actually announce that World War 3 has begun.

That I alone happened to learn of the war I put down to the curious character of the Reagan third term. It is no exaggeration to say that the United States, and much of the Western world, had deeply missed this amiable old actor who retired to California in 1989 after the inauguration of his luckless successor. The multiplication of the world's problems – the renewed energy crises, the second Iran/Iraq conflict, the destabilisation of the Soviet Union's Asiatic republics, the unnerving alliance in the USA between Islam and militant feminism – all prompted an intense nostalgia for the Reagan years. There was an immense affectionate memory of his gaffes and little incompetencies, his fondness (shared by those who elected him) for watching TV in his pyjamas rather than attending to more important matters, his confusion of reality with the half-remembered movies of his youth.

Tourists congregated in their hundreds outside the gates of the Reagans' retirement home in Bel Air, and occasionally the former President would totter out to pose on the porch. There, prompted by a still soignée Nancy, he would utter some amiable generality that brought tears to his listeners' eyes, and lifted both their hearts and stock markets around the world. As his successor's term in office drew to its unhappy close, the necessary constitutional amendment was swiftly passed through both Houses of Congress, with the express purpose of seeing that Reagan could enjoy his third term in the White House.

In January 1993 more than a million people turned out to cheer his inaugural drive through the streets of Washington, while the rest of the world watched on television. If the cathode eye could weep, it did so then.

Nonetheless, a few doubts remained, as the great political crises of the world stubbornly refused to be banished even by the aged President's ingratiating grin. The Iran/Iraq war threatened to embroil Turkey and Afghanistan. In defiance of the Kremlin, the Asiatic republics of the USSR were forming armed militias. Yves St-Laurent had designed the first chador for the power-dressing Islamicised feminists in the fashionable offices of Manhattan, London and Paris. Could even the Reagan Presidency cope with a world so askew?

Along with my fellow-physicians who had watched the President on television, I seriously doubted it. At this time, in the summer of 1994, Ronald Reagan was a man of eighty-three, showing all the signs of advancing senility. Like many old men, he enjoyed a few minutes each day of modest lucidity, during which he might utter some gnomic remark, and then lapse into a glassy twilight. His eyes were now too blurred to read the teleprompter, but his White House staff took advantage of the hearing aid he had always worn to insert a small speaker, so that he was able to recite his speeches by repeating like a child whatever he heard in his ear-piece. The pauses were edited out by the TV networks, but the hazards of remote control were revealed when the President, addressing the Catholic Mothers of America, startled the massed ranks of blue-rinsed ladies by suddenly repeating a studio engineer's aside: "Shift your ass, I gotta take a leak."

Watching this robotic figure with his eerie smiles and goofy grins, a few people began to ask if the President was brain-dead, or even alive at all. To reassure the nervous American public, unsettled by a falling stock market and by the news of armed insurrection in the Ukraine, the White House physicians began to release a series of regular reports on the President's health. A team of specialists at the

Walter Reed Hospital assured the nation that he enjoyed the robust physique and mental alertness of a man fifteen years his junior. Precise details of Reagan's blood pressure, his white and red cell counts, pulse and respiration were broadcast on TV and had an immediately calming effect. On the following day the world's stock markets showed a memorable lift, interest rates fell and Mr Gorbachev was able to announce that the Ukrainian separatists had moderated their demands.

Taking advantage of the unsuspected political asset represented by the President's bodily functions, the White House staff decided to issue their medical bulletins on a weekly basis. Not only did Wall Street respond positively, but opinion polls showed a strong recovery by the Republican Party as a whole. By the time of the mid-term Congressional elections, the medical reports were issued daily, and successful Republican candidates swept to control of both House and Senate thanks to an eve-of-poll bulletin on the regularity of the Presidential bowels.

From then on the American public was treated to a continuous stream of information on the President's health. Successive newscasts throughout the day would carry updates on the side-effects of a slight chill or the circulatory benefits of a dip in the White House pool. I well remember watching the news on Christmas Eve as my wife prepared our evening meal, and noticing that details of the President's health occupied five of the six leading news items.

"So his blood sugar is a little down," Susan remarked as she laid the festival table. "Good news for Quaker Oats and Pepsi."

"Really? Is there a connection, for heaven's sake?"

"Much more than you realise." She sat beside me on the sofa, pepper-mill in hand. "We'll have to wait for his latest urinalysis. It could be crucial."

"Dear, what's happening on the Pakistan border could be crucial. Gorbachev has threatened a pre-emptive strike against the rebel enclaves. The US has treaty obligations, theoretically a war could –"

"Sh . . ." Susan tapped my knee with the pepper-mill. "They've just run an Eysenck Personality Inventory – the old boy's scored full marks on emotional resonance and ability to relate. Results corrected for age, whatever that means."

"It means he's practically a basket case." I was about to change channels, hoping for some news of the world's real trouble spots, but a curious pattern had appeared along the bottom of the screen, some kind of Christmas decoration, I assumed, a line of stylised holly leaves. The rhythmic wave stabbed softly from left to right, accompanied by the soothing and nostalgic strains of "White Christmas".

"Good God . . ." Susan whispered in awe. "It's Ronnie's pulse. Did you hear the announcer? 'Transmitted live from the Heart of the Presidency'."

This was only the beginning. During the next few weeks, thanks to the miracle of modern radio-telemetry, the nation's TV screens became a scoreboard registering every detail of the President's physical and mental functions. His brave, if tremulous, heartbeat drew its trace along the lower edge of the screen, while above it newscasters expanded on his daily physical routines, on the twenty-eight feet he had walked in the rose garden, the calorie count of his modest lunches, the results of his latest brain-scan, read-outs of his kidney, liver and lung function. In addition, there was a daunting sequence of personality and IQ tests, all designed to reassure the American public that the man at the helm of the free world was more than equal to the daunting tasks that faced him across the Oval Office desk.

For all practical purposes, as I tried to explain to Susan, the President was scarcely more than a corpse wired for sound. I and my colleagues at the paediatric clinic were well aware of the old man's ordeal in submitting to this battery of tests. However, the White House staff knew that the American public was almost mesmerised by the spectacle of the President's heartbeat. The trace now ran below all other programmes, accompanying sit-coms, basketball matches and old World War 2 movies. Uncannily, its quickening beat would sometimes match the audience's own emotional responses, indicating that the President himself was watching

[27]

the same war films, including those in which he had appeared.

To complete the identification of President and TV screen – a consummation of which his political advisers had dreamed for so long – the White House staff arranged for further layers of information to be transmitted. Soon a third of the nation's TV screens were occupied by print-outs of heartbeat, blood pressure and EEG readings. Controversy briefly erupted when it became clear that delta waves predominated, confirming the long-held belief that the President was asleep for most of the day. However, the audiences were thrilled to know when Mr Reagan moved into REM sleep, the dream-time of the nation coinciding with that of its chief executive.

Untouched by this endless barrage of medical information, events in the real world continued down their perilous road. I bought every newspaper I could find, but their pages were dominated by graphic displays of the Reagan health bulletins and by expository articles outlining the significance of his liver enzyme functions and the slightest rise or fall in the concentration of the Presidential urine. Tucked away on the back pages I found a few brief references to civil war in the Asiatic republics of the Soviet Union, an attempted pro-Russian putsch in Pakistan, the Chinese invasion of Nepal, the mobilisation of NATO and Warsaw Pact reserves, the reinforcement of the US 5th and 7th Fleets.

But these ominous events, and the threat of a third world war, had the ill luck to coincide with a slight down-turn in the President's health. First reported on 20 January, this trivial cold caught by Reagan from a visiting grandchild drove all other news from the television screens. An army of reporters and film crews camped outside the White House, while a task force of specialists from the greatest research institutions in the land appeared in relays on every channel, interpreting the stream of medical data.

Like a hundred million Americans, Susan spent the next week sitting by the TV set, eyes following the print-out of the Reagan heartbeat.

"It's still only a cold," I reassured her when I returned from the clinic on 27 January. "What's the latest from Pakistan? There's a rumour that the Soviets have dropped paratroops into Karachi. The Delta force is moving from Subic Bay . . ."

[28]

"Not now!" She waved me aside, turning up the volume as an anchorman began yet another bulletin.

". . . here's an update on our report of two minutes ago. Good news on the President's CAT scan. There are no abnormal variations in the size or shape of the President's ventricles. Light rain is forecast for the D.C. area tonight, and the 8th Air Cavalry have exchanged fire with Soviet border patrols north of Kabul. We'll be back after the break with a report on the significance of that left temporal lobe spike . . ."

"For God's sake, there's no significance." I took the remote control unit from Susan's clenched hand and began to hunt the channels. "What about the Russian Baltic Fleet? The Kremlin is putting counter-pressure on NATO's northern flank. The US has to respond . . ."

By luck, I caught a leading network newscaster concluding a bulletin. He beamed confidently at the audience, his glamorous co-presenter smiling in anticipation.

". . . as of 5:05 Eastern Standard Time we can report that Mr Reagan's inter-cranial pressure is satisfactory. All motor and cognitive functions are normal for a man of the President's age. Repeat, motor and cognitive functions are normal. Now, here's a newsflash that's just reached us. At 2:35 local time President Reagan completed a satisfactory bowel motion." The newscaster turned to his co-presenter. "Barbara, I believe you have similar good news on Nancy?"

"Thank you, Dan," she cut in smoothly. "Yes, just one hour later, at 3:35 local time, Nancy completed her very own bowel motion, her second for the day, so it's all happening in the First Family." She glanced at a slip of paper pushed across her desk. "The traffic in Pennsylvania Avenue is seizing up again, while F-16s of the 6th Fleet have shot down seven MiG 29s over the Bering Strait. The President's blood pressure is 100 over 60. The ECG records a slight left-hand tremor . . ."

"A tremor of the left hand . . ." Susan repeated, clenching her fists. "Surely that's serious?"

I tapped the channel changer. "It could be. Perhaps he's thinking about having to press the nuclear button. Or else –"

An even more frightening possibility had occurred to me. I plunged through the medley of competing news bulletins, hoping to distract Susan as I glanced at the evening sky over Washington. The Soviet deep-water fleet patrolled 400 miles from the eastern coast of the United States. Soon mushroom clouds could be rising above the Pentagon.

". . . mild pituitary dysfunction is reported, and the President's physicians have expressed a modest level of concern. Repeat, a modest level of concern. The President convened the National Security Council some thirty minutes ago. SAC headquarters in Omaha, Nebraska, report all B-52 attack squadrons airborne. Now, I've just been handed a late bulletin from the White House Oncology Unit. A benign skin tumour was biopsied at 4:15 Washington time . . ."

". . . the President's physicians have again expressed their concern over Mr Reagan's calcified arteries and hardened cardiac valves. Hurricane Clara is now expected to bypass Puerto Rico, and the President has invoked the Emergency War Powers Act. After the break we'll have more expert analysis of Mr Reagan's retrograde amnesia. Remember, this condition can point to suspected Korsakoff syndrome . . ."

". . . psychomotor seizures, a distorted sense of time, colour changes and dizziness. Mr Reagan also reports an increased awareness of noxious odours. Other late news – blizzards cover the Midwest, and a state of war now exists between the United States and the Soviet Union. Stay tuned to this channel for a complete update on the President's brain metabolism . . ."

"We're at war," I said to Susan, and put my arms around her shoulders. But she was pointing to the erratic heart trace on the screen. Had the President suffered a brain storm and launched an all-out nuclear attack on the Russians? Were the incessant medical bulletins a clever camouflage to shield a volatile TV audience from the consequences of a desperate response to a national emergency? It would take only minutes for the Russian missiles to reach Washington, and I stared at the placid winter sky. Holding Susan in my arms, I listened to the cacophony of medical bulletins until, some four minutes later, I heard:

"... the President's physicians report dilated pupils and convulsive tremor, but neurochemical support systems are functioning adequately. The President's brain metabolism reveals increased glucose production. Scattered snow-showers are forecast overnight, and a cessation of hostilities has been agreed between the US and the USSR. After the break – the latest expert comment on that attack of Presidential flatulence. And why Nancy's left eyelid needed a tuck . . ."

I switched off the set and sat back in the strange silence. A small helicopter was crossing the grey sky over Washington. Almost as an afterthought, I said to Susan: "By the way, World War 3 has just ended."

Of course, Susan had no idea that the war had ever begun, a common failure among the public at large, as I realised over the next few weeks. Most people had only a vague recollection of the unrest in the Middle East. The news that nuclear bombs had landed in the deserted mountains of Alaska and eastern Siberia was lost in the torrent of medical reports that covered President Reagan's recovery from his cold.

In the second week of February 1995 I watched him on television as he presided over an American Legion ceremony on the White House lawn. His aged, ivory face was set in its familiar amiable grin, his eyes unfocused as he stood supported by two aides, the ever-watchful First Lady standing in her steely way beside him. Somewhere beneath the bulky black overcoat the radio-telemetry sensors transmitted the live print-outs of pulse, respiration and blood pressure that we could see on our screens. I guessed that the President, too, had forgotten that he had recently launched the Third World War. After all, no one had been killed, and in the public's mind the only possible casualty of those perilous hours had been Mr Reagan himself as he struggled to survive his cold.

Meanwhile, the world was a safer place. The brief nuclear

exchange had served its warning to the quarrelling factions around the planet. The secessionist movements in the Soviet Union had disbanded themselves, while elsewhere invading armies withdrew behind their frontiers. I could almost believe that World War 3 had been contrived by the Kremlin and the White House staff as a peacemaking device, and that the Reagan cold had been a diversionary trap into which the TV networks and newspapers had unwittingly plunged.

In tribute to the President's recuperative powers, the linear traces of his vital functions still notched their way across our TV screens. As he saluted the assembled veterans of the American Legion, I sensed the audience's collective pulse beating faster when the old actor's heart responded to the stirring sight of these marching men.

Then, among the Medal of Honor holders, I noticed a dishevelled young man in an ill-fitting uniform, out of step with his older companions. He pushed through the marching files as he drew a pistol from his tunic. There was a flurry of confusion while aides grappled with each other around the podium. The cameras swerved to catch the young man darting towards the President. Shots sounded above the wavering strains of the band. In the panic of uniformed men the President seemed to fall into the First Lady's arms and was swiftly borne away.

Searching the print-outs below the TV screen, I saw at once that the President's blood pressure had collapsed. The erratic pulse had levelled out into an unbroken horizontal line, and all respiratory function had ceased. It was only ten minutes later, as news was released of an unsuccessful assassination attempt, that the traces resumed their confident signatures.

Had the President died, perhaps for a second time? Had he, in a strict sense, ever lived during his third term of office? Will some animated spectre of himself, reconstituted from the medical print-outs that still parade across our TV screens, go on to yet further terms, unleashing fourth and fifth world wars, whose secret histories will expire within the interstices of our television schedules, forever lost within the ultimate urinalysis, the last great biopsy in the sky?

(1988)

[32]

Dream Cargoes

Across the lagoon an eager new life was forming, drawing its spectrum of colours from a palette more vivid than the sun's. Soon after dawn, when Johnson woke in Captain Galloway's cabin behind the bridge of the *Prospero*, he watched the lurid hues, cyanic blues and crimsons, playing against the ceiling above his bunk. Reflected in the metallic surface of the lagoon, the tropical foliage seemed to concentrate the Caribbean sunlight, painting on the warm air a screen of electric tones that Johnson had only seen on the nightclub façades of Miami and Vera Cruz.

He stepped onto the tilting bridge of the stranded freighter, aware that the island's vegetation had again surged forward during the night, as if it had miraculously found a means of converting darkness into these brilliant leaves and blossoms. Shielding his eyes from the glare, he searched the 600 yards of empty beach that encircled the *Prospero*, disappointed that there was no sign of Dr Chambers' rubber inflatable. For the past three mornings, when he woke after an uneasy night, he had seen the craft beached by the inlet of the lagoon. Shaking off the overlit dreams that rose from the contaminated waters, he would gulp down a cup of cold coffee, jump from the stern rail and set off between the pools of leaking chemicals in search of the American biologist.

It pleased Johnson that she was so openly impressed by this once barren island, a left-over of nature seven miles from the north-east coast of Puerto Rico. In his modest way he knew that he was responsible for the transformation of the nondescript atoll, scarcely more than a forgotten garbage dump left behind by the American army after World War 2. No-one, in Johnson's short life, had ever been

[33]

impressed by him, and the biologist's silent wonder gave him the first sense of achievement he had ever known.

Johnson had learned her name from the labels on the scientific stores in the inflatable. However, he had not yet approached or even spoken to her, embarrassed by his rough manners and shabby seaman's clothes, and the engrained chemical stench that banned him from sailors' bars all over the Caribbean. Now, when she failed to appear on the fourth morning, he regretted all the more that he had never worked up the courage to introduce himself.

Through the acid-streaked windows of the bridge-house he stared at the terraces of flowers that hung from the forest wall. A month earlier, when he first arrived at the island, struggling with the locked helm of the listing freighter, there had been no more than a few stunted palms growing among the collapsed army huts and water-tanks buried in the dunes.

But already, for reasons that Johnson preferred not to consider, a wholly new vegetation had sprung to life. The palms rose like flag-poles into the vivid Caribbean air, pennants painted with a fresh green sap. Around them the sandy floor was thick with flowering vines and ground ivy, blue leaves like dappled metal foil, as if some midnight gardener had watered them with a secret plant elixir as Johnson lay asleep in his bunk.

He put on Galloway's peaked cap and examined himself in the greasy mirror. Stepping onto the open deck behind the wheel-house, he inhaled the acrid chemical air of the lagoon. At least it masked the odours of the captain's cabin, a rancid bouquet of ancient sweat, cheap rum and diesel oil. He had thought seriously of abandoning Galloway's cabin and returning to his hammock in the forecastle, but despite the stench he felt that he owed it to himself to remain in the cabin. The moment that Galloway, with a last disgusted curse, had stepped into the freighter's single lifeboat he, Johnson, had become the captain of this doomed vessel.

He had watched Galloway, the four Mexican crewmen and the weary Portuguese engineer row off into the dusk, promising himself that he would sleep in the captain's cabin and take his meals at the captain's table. After five years at sea, working as cabin boy and deck hand on the lowest grade of chemical waste carrier, he had a command of his own, this antique freighter, even if the *Prospero*'s course was the vertical one to the sea-bed of the Caribbean.

Behind the funnel the Liberian flag of convenience hung in tatters, its fabric rotted by the acid air. Johnson stepped onto the stern ladder, steadying himself against the sweating hull-plates, and jumped into the shallow water. Careful to find his feet, he waded through the bilious green foam that leaked from the steel drums he had jettisoned from the freighter's deck.

When he reached the clear sand above the tide-line he wiped the emerald dye from his jeans and sneakers. Leaning to starboard in the lagoon, the *Prospero* resembled an exploded paint-box. The drums of chemical waste on the foredeck still dripped their effluent through the scuppers. The more sinister below-decks cargo – nameless organic by-products that Captain Galloway had been bribed to carry and never entered into his manifest – had dissolved the rusty plates and spilled an eerie spectrum of phosphorescent blues and indigos into the lagoon below.

Frightened of these chemicals, which every port in the Caribbean had rejected, Johnson had begun to jettison the cargo after running the freighter aground. But the elderly diesels had seized and the winch had jarred to a halt, leaving only a few of the drums on the nearby sand with their death's-head warnings and eroded seams.

Johnson set off along the shore, searching the sea beyond the inlet of the lagoon for any sign of Dr Chambers. Everywhere a deranged horticulture was running riot. Vivid new shoots pushed past the metal debris of old ammunition boxes, filing cabinets and truck tyres. Strange grasping vines clambered over the scarlet caps of giant fungi, their white stems as thick as sailors' bones. Avoiding them, Johnson walked towards an old staff car that sat in an open glade between the palms. Wheel-less, its military markings obliterated by the rain of decades, it had settled into the sand, vines encircling its roof and windshield.

Deciding to rest in the car, which once perhaps had driven an American general around the training camps of Puerto Rico, he tore away the vines that had wreathed themselves around the driver's door pillar. As he sat behind the steering wheel it occurred to Johnson that he might leave the freighter and set up camp on the island.

[35]

Nearby lay the galvanised iron roof of a barrack hut, enough material to build a beach house on the safer, seaward side of the island.

But Johnson was aware of an unstated bond between himself and the derelict freighter. He remembered the last desperate voyage of the *Prospero*, which he had joined in Vera Cruz, after being duped by Captain Galloway. The short voyage to Galveston, the debarkation port, would pay him enough to ship as a deck passenger on an inter-island boat heading for the Bahamas. It had been three years since he had seen his widowed mother in Nassau, living in a plywood bungalow by the airport with her invalid boyfriend.

Needless to say, they had never berthed at Galveston, Miami or any other of the ports where they had tried to unload their cargo. The crudely sealed cylinders of chemical waste-products, supposedly en route to a reprocessing plant in southern Texas, had begun to leak before they left Vera Cruz. Captain Galloway's temper, like his erratic seamanship and consumption of rum and tequila, increased steadily as he realised that the Mexican shipping agent had abandoned them to the seas. Almost certainly the agent had pocketed the monies allocated for reprocessing and found it more profitable to let the ancient freighter, now refused entry to Vera Cruz, sail up and down the Gulf of Mexico until her corroded keel sent her conveniently to the bottom.

For two months they had cruised forlornly from one port to another, boarded by hostile maritime police and customs officers, public health officials and journalists alerted to the possibility of a major ecological disaster. At Kingston, Jamaica, a television launch trailed them to the ten-mile limit, at Santo Domingo a spotter plane of the Dominican navy was waiting for them when they tried to slip into harbour under the cover of darkness. Greenpeace power-boats intercepted them outside Tampa, Florida, when Captain Galloway tried to dump part of his cargo. Firing flares across the bridge of the freighter, the US Coast Guard dispatched them into the Gulf of Mexico in time to meet the tail of Hurricane Clara.

When at last they recovered from the storm the cargo had shifted, and the *Prospero* listed ten degrees to starboard. Fuming chemicals leaked across the decks from the fractured seams of the waste drums, boiled on the surface of the sea and sent up a cloud of acrid vapour that left Johnson and the Mexican crewmen coughing through makeshift face-masks, and Captain Galloway barricading himself into his cabin with his tequila bottle.

First Officer Pereira had saved the day, rigging up a hose-pipe that sprayed the leaking drums with a torrent of water, but by then the *Prospero* was taking in the sea through its strained plates. When they sighted Puerto Rico the captain had not even bothered to set a course for port. Propping himself against the helm, a bottle in each hand, he signalled Pereira to cut the engines. In a self-pitying monologue, he cursed the Mexican shipping agent, the US Coast Guard, the world's agro-chemists and their despicable science that had deprived him of his command. Lastly he cursed Johnson for being so foolish ever to step aboard this ill-fated ship. As the *Prospero* lay doomed in the water, Pereira appeared with his already packed suitcase, and the captain ordered the Mexicans to lower the life-boat.

It was then that Johnson made his decision to remain on board. All his life he had failed to impose himself on anything – running errands as a six-year-old for the Nassau airport shoe-blacks, cadging pennies for his mother from the irritated tourists, enduring the years of school where he had scarcely learned to read and write, working as a dishwasher at the beach restaurants, forever conned out of his wages by the thieving managers. He had always reacted to events, never initiated anything on his own. Now, for the first time, he could become the captain of the *Prospero* and master of his own fate. Long before Galloway's curses faded into the dusk Johnson had leapt down the companionway ladder into the engine room.

As the elderly diesels rallied themselves for the last time Johnson returned to the bridge. He listened to the propeller's tired but steady beat against the dark ocean, and slowly turned the *Prospero* towards the north-west. Five hundred miles away were the Bahamas, and an endless archipelago of secret harbours. Somehow he would get rid of the leaking drums and even, perhaps, ply for hire between the islands, renaming the old tub after his mother, Velvet Mae. Meanwhile Captain Johnson stood proudly on the bridge, oversize cap on his head, 300 tons of steel deck obedient beneath his feet.

By dawn the next day he was completely lost on an open sea. During the night the freighter's list had increased. Below decks the leaking chemicals had etched their way through the hull plates, and a phosphorescent steam enveloped the bridge. The engine room was a knee-deep vat of acid brine, a poisonous vapour rising through the ventilators and coating every rail and deck-plate with a lurid slime.

Then, as Johnson searched desperately for enough timber to build a raft, he saw the old World War 2 garbage island seven miles from the Puerto Rican coast. The lagoon inlet was unguarded by the US Navy or Greenpeace speedboats. He steered the *Prospero* across the calm surface and let the freighter settle into the shallows. The inrush of water smothered the cargo in the hold. Able to breathe again, Johnson rolled into Captain Galloway's bunk, made a space for himself among the empty bottles and slept his first dreamless sleep.

"Hey, you! Are you all right?" A woman's hand pounded on the roof of the staff car. "What *are* you doing in there?"

Johnson woke with a start, lifting his head from the steering wheel. While he slept the lianas had enveloped the car, climbing up the roof and windshield pillars. Vivid green tendrils looped themselves around his left hand, tying his wrist to the rim of the wheel.

Wiping his face, he saw the American biologist peering at him through the leaves, as if he were the inmate of some bizarre zoo whose cages were the bodies of abandoned motor-cars. He tried to free himself, and pushed against the driver's door.

"Sit back! I'll cut you loose."

She slashed at the vines with her clasp knife, revealing her fierce and determined wrist. When Johnson stepped onto the ground she held his shoulders, looking him up and down with a thorough eye. She was no more than thirty, three years older than himself, but to Johnson she seemed as self-possessed and remote as the Nassau school-teachers. Yet her mouth was more relaxed than those pursed lips of his childhood, as if she were genuinely concerned for Johnson.

"You're all right," she informed him. "But I wouldn't go for too many rides in that car."

She strolled away from Johnson, her hands pressing the burnished copper trunks of the palms, feeling the urgent pulse of awakening life. Around her shoulders was slung a canvas bag holding a clip-board, sample jars, a camera and reels of film.

"My name's Christine Chambers," she called out to Johnson. "I'm carrying out a botanical project on this island. Have you come from the stranded ship?"

"I'm the captain," Johnson told her without deceit. He reached into the car and retrieved his peaked cap from the eager embrace of the vines, dusted it off and placed it on his head at what he hoped was a rakish angle. "She's not a wreck – I beached her here for repairs."

"Really? For repairs?" Christine Chambers watched him archly, finding him at least as intriguing as the giant scarlet-capped fungi. "So you're the captain. But where's the crew?"

"They abandoned ship." Johnson was glad that he could speak so honestly. He liked this attractive biologist and the way she took a close interest in the island. "There were certain problems with the cargo."

"I bet there were. You were lucky to get here in one piece." She took out a notebook and jotted down some observation on Johnson, glancing at his pupils and lips. "Captain, would you like a sandwich? I've brought a picnic lunch – you look as if you could use a square meal."

"Well . . ." Pleased by her use of his title, Johnson followed her to the beach, where the inflatable sat on the sand. Clearly she had been delayed by the weight of stores: a bell tent, plastic coolers, cartons of canned food, and a small office cabinet. Johnson had survived on a diet of salt beef, cola and oatmeal biscuits he cooked on the galley stove.

For all the equipment, she was in no hurry to unload the stores, as if unsure of sharing the island with Johnson, or perhaps pondering a different approach to her project, one that involved the participation of the human population of the island.

Trying to reassure her as they divided the sandwiches, he described the last voyage of the *Prospero*, and the disaster of the leak-ing chemicals. She nodded while he spoke, as if she already knew something of the story.

"It sounds to me like a great feat of seamanship," she complimented him. "The crew who abandoned ship – as it happens, they reported that she went down near Barbados. One of them, Galloway I think he was called, claimed they'd spent a month in an open boat."

"Galloway?" Johnson assumed the pursed lips of the Nassau school-marms. "One of my less reliable men. So no-one is looking for the ship?"

"No. Absolutely no-one."

"And they think she's gone down?"

"Right to the bottom. Everyone in Barbados is relieved there's no pollution. Those tourist beaches, you know."

"They're important. And no-one in Puerto Rico thinks she's here?"

"No-one except me. This island is my research project," she explained. "I teach biology at San Juan University, but I really want to work at Harvard. I can tell you, lectureships are hard to come by. Something very interesting is happening here, with a little luck . . ."

"It is interesting," Johnson agreed. There was a conspiratorial note to Dr Christine's voice that made him uneasy. "A lot of old army equipment is buried here – I'm thinking of building a house on the beach."

"A good idea . . . even if it takes you four or five months. I'll help you out with any food you need. But be careful." Dr Christine pointed to the weal on his arm, a temporary reaction against some invading toxin in the vine sap. "There's something else that's interesting about this island, isn't there?"

"Well . . ." Johnson stared at the acid stains etching through the *Prospero*'s hull and spreading across the lagoon. He had tried not to think of his responsibility for these dangerous and unstable chemicals. "There are a few other things going on here."

"A few other things?" Dr Christine lowered her voice. "Look, Johnson, you're sitting in the middle of an amazing biological experiment. No-one would allow it to happen anywhere in the world – if they knew, the US Navy would move in this afternoon."

"Would they take away the ship?"

"They'd take it away and sink it in the nearest ocean trench, then scorch the island with flame-throwers."

"And what about me?"

[40]

"I wouldn't like to say. It might depend on how advanced . . ." She held his shoulder reassuringly, aware that her vehemence had shocked him. "But there's no reason why they should find out. Not for a while, and by then it won't matter. I'm not exaggerating when I say that you've probably created a new kind of life."

As they unloaded the stores Johnson reflected on her words. He had guessed that the chemicals leaking from the *Prospero* had set off the accelerated growth, and that the toxic reagents might equally be affecting himself. In Galloway's cabin mirror he inspected the hairs on his chin and any suspicious moles. The weeks at sea, inhaling the acrid fumes, had left him with raw lungs and throat, and an erratic appetite, but he had felt better since coming ashore.

He watched Christine step into a pair of thigh-length rubber boots and move into the shallow water, ladle in hand, looking at the plant and animal life of the lagoon. She filled several specimen jars with the phosphorescent water, and locked them into the cabinet inside the tent.

"Johnson – you couldn't let me see the cargo manifest?"

"Captain . . . Galloway took it with him. He didn't list the real cargo."

"I bet he didn't." Christine pointed to the vermilion-shelled crabs that scuttled through the vivid filaments of kelp, floating like threads of blue electric cable. "Have you noticed? There are no dead fish or crabs – and you'd expect to see hundreds. That was the first thing I spotted. And it isn't just the crabs – you look pretty healthy . . ."

"Maybe I'll be stronger?" Johnson flexed his sturdy shoulders.

". . . in a complete daze, mentally, but I imagine that will change. Meanwhile, can you take me on board? I'd like to visit the *Prospero*."

"Dr Christine . . ." Johnson held her arm, trying to restrain this determined woman. He looked at her clear skin and strong legs. "It's too dangerous, you might fall through the deck."

"Fair enough. Are the containers identified?"

"Yes, there's no secret." Johnson did his best to remember. "Organo . . ."

"Organo-phosphates? Right – what I need to know is which

containers are leaking and roughly how much. We might be able to work out the exact chemical reactions – you may not realise it, Johnson, but you've mixed a remarkably potent cocktail. A lot of people will want to learn the recipe, for all kinds of reasons . . ."

Sitting in the colonel's chair on the porch of the beach-house, Johnson gazed contentedly at the luminous world around him, a fever-realm of light and life that seemed to have sprung from his own mind. The jungle wall of cycads, giant tamarinds and tropical creepers crowded the beach to the waterline, and the reflected colours drowned in swathes of phosphorescence that made the lagoon resemble a cauldron of electric dyes.

So dense was the vegetation that almost the only free sand lay below Johnson's feet. Every morning he would spend an hour cutting back the flowering vines and wild magnolia that inundated the metal shack. Already the foliage was crushing the galvanised iron roof. However hard he worked – and he found himself too easily distracted – he had been unable to keep clear the inspection pathways which Christine patrolled on her weekend visits, camera and specimen jars at the ready.

Hearing the sound of her inflatable as she neared the inlet of the lagoon, Johnson surveyed his domain with pride. He had found a metal card-table buried in the sand, and laid it with a selection of fruits he had picked for Christine that morning. To Johnson's untrained eye they seemed to be strange hybrids of pomegranate and pawpaw, cantaloupe and pineapple. There were giant tomato-like berries and clusters of purple grapes each the size of a baseball. Together they glowed through the overheated light like jewels set in the face of the sun.

By now, four months after his arrival on the *Prospero*, the one-time garbage island had become a unique botanical garden, generating new species of trees, vines and flowering plants every day. A powerful life-engine was driving the island. As she crossed the lagoon in her inflatable Christine stared at the aerial terraces of vines and blossoms that had sprung up since the previous weekend.

The dead hulk of the *Prospero*, daylight visible through its acid-etched plates, sat in the shallow water, the last of its chemical wastes leaking into the lagoon. But Johnson had forgotten the ship and the voyage that had brought him here, just as he had forgotten his past life and unhappy childhood under the screaming engines of Nassau airport. Lolling back in his canvas chair, on which was stencilled "Colonel Pottle, US Army Engineer Corps", he felt like a plantation owner who had successfully subcontracted a corner of the original Eden. As he stood up to greet Christine he thought only of the future, of his pregnant bride and the son who would soon share the island with him.

"Johnson! My God, what have you been doing?" Christine ran the inflatable onto the beach and sat back, exhausted by the buffeting waves. "It's a botanical mad-house!"

Johnson was so pleased to see her that he forgot his regret over their weekly separations. As she explained, she had her student classes to teach, her project notes and research samples to record and catalogue.

"Dr Christine . . . ! I waited all day!" He stepped into the shallow water, a carmine surf filled with glowing animalcula, and pulled the inflatable onto the sand. He helped her from the craft, his eyes avoiding her curving abdomen under the smock.

"Go on, you can stare . . ." Christine pressed his hand to her stomach. "How do I look, Johnson?"

"Too beautiful for me, and the island. We've all gone quiet."

"That is gallant – you've become a poet, Johnson."

Johnson never thought of other women, and knew that none could be so beautiful as this lady biologist bearing his child. He spotted a plastic cooler among the scientific equipment.

"Christine – you've brought me ice-cream . . ."

"Of course I have. But don't eat it yet. We've a lot to do, Johnson."

He unloaded the stores, leaving to the last the nylon nets and spring-mounted steel frames in the bottom of the boat. These bird-traps were the one cargo he hated to unload. Nesting in the highest branches above the island was a flock of extravagant aerial creatures, sometime swallows and finches whose jewelled plumage and tail-fans transformed them into gaudy peacocks. He had set the traps reluctantly at Christine's insistence. He never objected to catching

[43]

the phosphorescent fish with their enlarged fins and ruffs of external gills, which seemed to prepare them for life on the land, or the crabs and snails in their baroque armour. But the thought of Christine taking these rare and beautiful birds back to her laboratory made him uneasy – he guessed that they would soon end their days under the dissection knife.

"Did you set the traps for me, Johnson?"

"I set all of them and put in the bait."

"Good." Christine heaped the nets onto the sand. More and more she seemed to hurry these days, as if she feared that the experiment might end. "I can't understand why we haven't caught one of them."

Johnson gave an eloquent shrug. In fact he had eaten the canned sardines, and released the one bird that had strayed into the trap below the parasol of a giant cycad. The nervous creature with its silken scarlet wings and kite-like tail feathers had been a dream of flight. "Nothing yet – they're clever, those birds."

"Of course they are – they're a new species." She sat in Colonel Pottle's chair, photographing the table of fruit with her small camera. "Those grapes are huge – I wonder what sort of wine they'd make. Champagne of the gods, grand cru . . ."

Warily, Johnson eyed the purple and yellow globes. He had eaten the fish and crabs from the lagoon, when asked by Christine, with no ill effects, but he was certain that these fruits were intended for the birds. He knew that Christine was using him, like everything else on the island, as part of her experiment. Even the child she had conceived after their one brief act of love, over so quickly that he was scarcely sure it had ever occurred, was part of the experiment. Perhaps the child would be the first of a new breed of man and he, Johnson, errand runner for airport shoe-shine boys, would be the father of an advanced race that would one day repopulate the planet.

As if aware of his impressive physique, she said: "You look wonderfully well, Johnson. If this experiment ever needs to be justified . . ."

"I'm very strong now – I'll be able to look after you and the boy."

"It might be a girl – or something in between." She spoke in a matter-of-fact way that always surprised him. "Tell me, Johnson, what do you do while I'm away?"

"I think about you, Dr Christine."

"And I certainly think about you. But do you sleep a lot?"

"No. I'm busy with my thoughts. The time goes very quickly."

Christine casually opened her note-pad. "You mean the hours go by without you noticing?"

"Yes. After breakfast I fill the oil-lamp and suddenly it's time for lunch. But it can go more slowly, too. If I look at a falling leaf in a certain way it seems to stand still."

"Good. You're learning to control time. Your mind is enlarging, Johnson."

"Maybe I'll be as clever as you, Dr Christine."

"Ah, I think you're moving in a much more interesting direction. In fact, Johnson, I'd like you to eat some of the fruit. Don't worry, I've already analysed it, and I'll have some myself." She was cutting slices of the melon-sized apple. "I want the baby to try some."

Johnson hesitated, but as Christine always reminded him, none of the new species had revealed a single deformity.

The fruit was pale and sweet, with a pulpy texture and a tang like alcoholic mango. It slightly numbed Johnson's mouth and left a pleasant coolness in the stomach.

A diet for those with wings.

"Johnson! Are you sick?"

He woke with a start, not from sleep but from an almost too-clear examination of the colour patterns of a giant butterfly that had settled on his hand. He looked up from his chair at Christine's concerned eyes, and at the dense vines and flowering creepers that crowded the porch, pressing against his shoulders. The amber of her eyes was touched by the same overlit spectrum that shone through the trees and blossoms. Everything on the island was becoming a prism of itself.

"Johnson, wake up!"

"I am awake. Christine . . . I didn't hear you come."

"I've been here for an hour." She touched his cheeks, searching for any sign of fever and puzzled by Johnson's distracted manner. Behind her, the inflatable was beached on the few feet of sand not smothered by the vegetation. The dense wall of palms, lianas and flowering plants had collapsed onto the shore. Engorged on the sun, the giant fruits had begun to split under their own weight, and streams of vivid juice ran across the sand, as if the forest were bleeding.

"Christine? You came back so soon . . . ?" It seemed to Johnson that she had left only a few minutes earlier. He remembered waving goodbye to her and sitting down to finish his fruit and admire the giant butterfly, its wings like the painted hands of a circus clown.

"Johnson – I've been away for a week." She held his shoulder, frowning at the unstable wall of rotting vegetation that towered a hundred feet into the air. Cathedrals of flower-decked foliage were falling into the waters of the lagoon.

"Johnson, help me to unload the stores. You don't look as if you've eaten for days. Did you trap the birds?"

"Birds? No, nothing yet." Vaguely Johnson remembered setting the traps, but he had been too distracted by the wonder of everything to pursue the birds. Graceful, feather-tipped wraiths like gaudy angels, their crimson plumage leaked its ravishing hues onto the air. When he fixed his eyes onto them they seemed suspended against the sky, wings fanning slowly as if shaking the time from themselves.

He stared at Christine, aware that the colours were separating themselves from her skin and hair. Superimposed images of herself, each divided from the others by a fraction of a second, blurred the air around her, an exotic plumage that sprang from her arms and shoulders. The staid reality that had trapped them all was beginning to dissolve. Time had stopped and Christine was ready to rise into the air . . .

He would teach Christine and the child to fly.

"Christine, we can all learn."

"What, Johnson?"

"We can learn to fly. There's no time any more – everything's too beautiful for time."

"Johnson, look at my watch."

"We'll go and live in the trees, Christine. We'll live with the high flowers . . ."

He took her arm, eager to show her the mystery and beauty of the sky people they would become. She tried to protest, but gave in, humouring Johnson as he led her gently from the beach house to the wall of inflamed flowers. Her hand on the radio-transmitter in the inflatable, she sat beside the crimson lagoon as Johnson tried to climb the flowers towards the sun. Steadying the child within her, she wept for Johnson, only calming herself two hours later when the siren of a naval cutter crossed the inlet.

"I'm glad you radioed in," the US Navy lieutenant told Christine. "One of the birds reached the base at San Juan. We tried to keep it alive but it was crushed by the weight of its own wings. Like everything else on this island."

He pointed from the bridge to the jungle wall. Almost all the over-crowded canopy had collapsed into the lagoon, leaving behind only a few of the original palms with their bird traps. The blossoms glowed through the water like thousands of drowned lanterns.

"How long has the freighter been here?" An older civilian, a government scientist holding a pair of binoculars, peered at the riddled hull of the *Prospero*. Below the beach house two sailors were loading the last of Christine's stores into the inflatable. "It looks as if it's been stranded there for years."

"Six months," Christine told him. She sat beside Johnson, smiling at him encouragingly. "When Captain Johnson realised what was going on he asked me to call you."

"Only six? That must be roughly the life-cycle of these new species. Their cellular clocks seem to have stopped – instead of reproducing, they force-feed their own tissues, like those giant fruit that contain no seeds. The life of the individual becomes the entire life of the species." He gestured towards the impassive Johnson. "That probably explains our friend's altered time sense – great blocks of memory were coalescing in his mind, so that a ball thrown into the air would never appear to land . . ."

A tide of dead fish floated past the cutter's bow, the gleaming bodies like discarded costume jewellery.

"You weren't contaminated in any way?" the lieutenant asked Christine. "I'm thinking of the baby."

[47]

"No, I didn't eat any of the fruit," Christine said firmly. "I've been here only twice, for a few hours."

"Good. Of course, the medical people will do all the tests."

"And the island?"

"We've been ordered to torch the whole place. The demolition charges are timed to go off in just under two hours, but we'll be well out of range. It's a pity, in a way."

"The birds are still here," Christine said, aware of Johnson staring at the trees.

"Luckily, you've trapped them all." The scientist offered her the binoculars. "Those organic wastes are hazardous things - God knows what might happen if human beings were exposed to long-term contact. All sorts of sinister alterations to the nervous system - people might be happy to stare at a stone all day."

Johnson listened to them talking, glad to feel Christine's hand in his own. She was watching him with a quiet smile, aware that they shared the conspiracy. She would try to save the child, the last fragment of the experiment, and he knew that if it survived it would face a fierce challenge from those who feared it might replace them.

But the birds endured. His head had cleared, and he remembered the visions that had given him a brief glimpse of another, more advanced world. High above the collapsed canopy of the forest he could see the traps he had set, and the great crimson birds sitting on their wings. At least they could carry the dream forward.

Ten minutes later, when the inflatable had been winched onto the deck, the cutter set off through the inlet. As it passed the western headland the lieutenant helped Christine towards the cabin. Johnson followed them, then pushed aside the government scientist and leapt from the rail, diving cleanly into the water. He struck out for the shore a hundred feet away, knowing that he was strong enough to climb the trees and release the birds, with luck a mating pair who would take him with them in their escape from time.

(1991)

The Object of the Attack

*From the Forensic Diaries of Dr Richard Greville,
Chief Psychiatric Adviser, Home Office*

7 June 1987. An unsettling week – two Select Committees; the failure of mother's suspect Palmer to reach its reserve at Sotheby's (I suggested that they might re-attribute it to Keating, which doubly offended them); and wearying arguments with Sarah about our endlessly postponed divorce and her over-reliance on ECT – she is strongly for the former, I as strongly against the latter . . . I suspect that her patients are suffering for me.

But, above all, there was my visit to The Boy. Confusing, ugly and yet strangely inspiring. Inviting me to Daventry, Governor Henson referred to him, as does everyone else in the Home Office, as "the boy", but I feel he has now earned the capital letters. Years of being moved about, from Rampton to Broadmoor to the Home Office Special Custody Unit at Daventry, the brutal treatment and solitary confinement have failed to subdue him.

He stood in the shower stall of the punishment wing, wearing full canvas restraint suit, and plainly driven mad by the harsh light reflected from the white tiles, which were streaked with blood from a leaking contusion on his forehead. He has been punched about a great deal, and flinched from me as I approached, but I felt that he almost invited physical attack as a means of provoking himself. He is far smaller than I expected, and looks only seventeen or eighteen (though he is now twenty-nine), but is still strong and dangerous – President Reagan and Her Majesty were probably lucky to escape.

Case notes: missing caps to both canines, contact dermatitis of the scalp, a left-handed intention tremor, and signs of an hysterical photophobia. He appeared to be gasping with fear, and Governor Henson tried to reassure him, but I assume that far from being afraid he felt nothing but contempt for us and was deliberately hyperventilating. He was chanting what sounded like "Allahu akbar", the expulsive God-is-Great cry used by the whirling dervishes to induce their hallucinations, the same over-oxygenation of the brain brought on, in milder form, by church hymns and community singing at Cup Finals.

The Boy certainly resembles a religious fanatic – perhaps he is a Shi'ite Muslim convert? He only paused to stare at the distant aerials of Daventry visible through a skylight. When a warder closed the door he began to whimper and pump his lungs again. I asked the orderly to clean the wound on his forehead, but as I helped with the dressing he lunged forward and knocked my briefcase to the floor. For a few seconds he tried to provoke an assault, but then caught sight of the Sotheby's catalogue among my spilled papers, and the reproduction of mother's Samuel Palmer. That serene light over the visionary meadows, the boughs of the oaks like windows of stained glass in the cathedral of heaven, together appeared to calm him. He gazed at me in an uncanny way, bowing as if he assumed that I was the painter.

Later, in the Governor's office, we came to the real purpose of my visit. The months of disruptive behaviour have exhausted everyone, but above all they are terrified of an escape, and a second attack on HMQ. Nor would it help the Atlantic Alliance if the US President were assassinated by a former inmate of a British mental hospital. Henson and the resident medical staff, with the encouragement of the Home Office, are keen to switch from chlorpromazine to the new NX series of central nervous system depressants – a spin-off of Porton Down's work on nerve gases. Prolonged use would induce blurred vision and locomotor ataxia, but also suppress all cortical function, effectively lobotomising him. I thought of my wrangles with Sarah over ECT – psychiatry cannot wait to return to its dark ages – and tactfully vetoed the use of NX until I had studied the medical history in the Special Branch dossier. But I was thinking of The Boy's eyes as he gazed on that dubious Palmer.

[50]

In 1982, during the state visit of President Reagan to the United Kingdom, an unsuccessful aerial attack was made upon the royal family and their guest at Windsor Castle. Soon after the President and Mrs Reagan arrived by helicopter, a miniature glider was observed flying across the Home Park in a north-westerly direction. The craft, a primitive hang-glider, was soaring at a height of some 120 feet, on a course that would have carried it over the walls of the Castle. However, before the Special Branch and Secret Service marksmen could fire upon the glider it became entangled in the aerials above the royal mausoleum at Frogmore House and fell to the ground beside the Long Walk.

Strapped to the chest of the unconscious pilot was an explosive harness containing twenty-four sticks of commercial gelignite linked to NCB detonators, and a modified parachute ripcord that served as a hand-operated triggering device. The pilot was taken into custody, and no word of this presumed assassination attempt was released to the public or to the Presidential party. HMQ alone was informed, which may explain Her Majesty's impatience with the President when, on horseback, he paused to exchange banter with a large group of journalists.

The pilot was never charged or brought to trial, but detained under the mental health acts in the Home Office observation unit at Springfield Hospital. He was a twenty-four-year-old former video-games programmer and failed Jesuit novice named Matthew Young. For the past eight months he had been living in a lock-up garage behind a disused Baptist church in Highbury, north London, where he had constructed his flying machine. Squadron Leader D. H. Walsh of the RAF Museum, Hendon, identified the craft as an exact replica of a glider designed by the 19th-century aviation pioneer Otto Lilienthal. Later research showed that the glider was the craft in which Lilienthal met his death in 1896. Fellow-residents in the lock-up garages, former girlfriends of the would-be assassin, and his probation officer, all witnessed his construction of the glider during the spring of 1982. However, how he launched this antique machine – the nearest high ground is the Heathrow control tower five miles to the east – or remained airborne for his flight across the Home Park is a mystery to this day.

Later, in the interview cell, The Boy sat safely handcuffed between his two warders. The bruised and hyperventilating figure had been replaced by a docile youth resembling a reformed skinhead who had miraculously seen the light. Only the eerie smile which he turned upon me so obligingly reminded me of the glider and the harness packed with explosive. As always, he refused to answer any questions put to him, and we sat in a silence broken only by his whispered refrain.

Ignoring these cryptic mutterings, I studied a list of those present at Windsor Castle.

> President Reagan, HM the Queen, Mrs Reagan, Prince Philip, Prince Charles, Princess Diana . . .
>
> The US Ambassador, Dr Billy Graham, Apollo astronaut Colonel Tom Stamford, Mr Henry Ford III, Mr James Stewart, the presidents of Heinz, IBM and Lockheed Aircraft, and assorted Congressmen, military and naval attachés, State Department and CIA pro-consuls . . .
>
> Lord Delfont, Mr Andrew Lloyd Webber, Miss Joanna Lumley . . .

In front of Young, on the table between us, I laid out the photographs of President Reagan, the Queen, Prince Philip, Charles and Diana. He showed not a flicker of response, leaned forward and with his scarred chin nudged the Sotheby's catalogue from my open briefcase. He held the Palmer reproduction to his left shoulder, obliquely smiling his thanks. Sly and disingenuous, he was almost implying that I was his accomplice. I remembered how very manipulative such psychopaths could be – Myra Hindley, Brady and Mary Bell had convinced various naïve and well-meaning souls of their "religious conversions".

Without thinking, I drew the last photograph from the dossier:

Colonel Stamford in his white space-suit floating free above a space craft during an orbital flight.

The chanting stopped. I heard Young's heels strike the metal legs of his chair as he drew back involuntarily. A focal seizure of the right hand rattled his handcuffs. He stared at the photograph, but the gaze of his eyes was far beyond the cell around us, and I suspected that he was experiencing a warning aura before an epileptic attack. With a clear shout to us all, he stiffened in his chair and slipped to the floor in a *grand mal*.

As his head hammered the warders' feet I realised that he had been chanting, not "Allahu akbar", but "Astro-naut" . . .

Astro-nought . . . ?

Matthew Young: The Personal History of a Psychopath

So, what is known of The Boy? The Special Branch investigators assembled a substantial dossier on this deranged young man.

Born 1958, Abu Dhabi, father manager of Amoco desalination plant. Childhood in the Gulf area, Alaska and Aberdeen. Educational misfit, with suspected *petit mal* epilepsy, but attended Strathclyde University for two terms in 1975, computer sciences course. Joined Workers' Revolutionary Party 1976, arrested outside US Embassy, London, during anti-nuclear demonstration. Worked as scaffolder and painter, Jodrell Bank Radio-Observatory, 1977; prosecuted for malicious damage to reflector dish. Jesuit novice, St Francis Xavier seminary, Dundalk, 1978; expelled after three weeks for sexual misconduct with mother of fellow novice. Fined for being drunk and disorderly during "Sculpture of the Space Age" exhibition at Serpentine Gallery, London. Video-games programmer, Virgin Records, 1980. Operated pirate radio station attempting to jam transmissions from Space Shuttle, prosecuted by British Telecom. Registered private patents on video-games "Target Apollo" and "Shuttle Attack", 1981. Numerous convictions for assault, possession of narcotics, dangerous driving, unemployment benefit frauds, disturbances of the peace. 1982, privately published his "Cosmological Testament", a Blakean farrago of nature mysticism, apocalyptic fantasy and pseudo-mathematical proofs of the non-existence of space-time . . .

All in all, a classic delinquent, with that history of messianic delusions and social maladjustment found in regicides throughout history. The choice of Mr Reagan reflects the persistent appeal of the theme of Presidential assassination, which seems to play on the edgy dreams of so many lonely psychopaths. Invested in the President of the United States, the world's most powerful leader, are not only the full office and authority of the temporal world, but the very notion of existence itself, of the continuum of time and space which encloses the assassin as much as his victim. Like the disturbed child seeking to destroy everything in its nursery, the assassin is trying to obliterate those images of himself which he identifies with his perception of the external universe. Suicide would leave the rest of existence intact, and it is the notion of existence, incarnated in the person of the President, that is the assassin's true target.

The Dream of Death by Air

". . . in the Second Fall, their attempt to escape from their home planet, the peoples of the earth invite their planetary death, choosing the zero gravity of a false space and time, recapitulating in their weightlessness the agony of the First Fall of Man . . ."

COSMOLOGICAL TESTAMENT, BOOK I

The Dream of Death by Water

". . . the sea is an exposed cerebral cortex, the epidermis of a sleeping giant whom the Apollo and Skylab astronauts will awake with their splashdowns. All the peoples of the planet will walk, fly, entrain for the nearest beach, they will ride rapids, endure hardships, abandon continents until they at last stand together on the terminal shore of the world, then step forward . . ."

COSMOLOGICAL TESTAMENT, BOOK III

The Dream of Death by Earth

". . . the most sinister and dangerous realms are those devised by man during his inward colonising of his planet, applying the dreams of a degenerate outer space to his inner world – warrens, dungeons, fortifications, bunkers, oubliettes, underground garages, tunnels of every kind that riddle his mind like maggots through the brains of a corpse . . ." COSMOLOGICAL TESTAMENT, BOOK VII

A curious volume, certainly, but no hint of a dream of death by fire – and no suggestion of Reagan, nor of Her Majesty, Princess Diana, Mrs Thatcher . . . ?

The Escape Engine: The Ames Room

14 October 1987. The Boy has escaped! An urgent call this morning from Governor Henson. I flew up to Daventry immediately in the crowded Home Office helicopter. Matthew Young has vanished, in what must be one of the most ingenious escape attempts ever devised. The Governor and his staff were in a disoriented state when I arrived. Henson paced around his office, pressing his hands against the bookshelves and re-arranging the furniture, as if not trusting its existence. Home Office and Special Branch people were everywhere, but I managed to calm Henson and piece together the story.

Since my previous visit they had relaxed Young's regime. Mysteriously, the Samuel Palmer illustration in Sotheby's catalogue had somehow calmed him. He no longer defaced his cell walls, volunteered to steamhose them, and had pinned the Palmer above his bunk, gazing at it as if it were a religious icon. (If only it were a Keating – the old rogue would have been delighted. As it happens, Keating's reputation as a faker may have given Young his plan for escape.)

Young declined to enter the exercise yard – the high British Telecom aerials clearly unsettled him – so Henson arranged for him to use the prison chapel as a recreation room. Here the trouble began, as became clear when the Governor showed me into the chapel, a former private cinema furnished with pews, altar, pulpit, etc. For reasons of security, the doors were kept locked, and the warders on duty kept their eyes on Young by glancing through the camera slit in the projection room. As a result, the warders saw the interior of the chapel from one perspective only. Young had cunningly taken advantage of this, re-arranging the pews, pulpit and altar table to construct what in effect was an Ames Room – Adelbert Ames Jr, the American psychologist, devised a series of trick rooms, which seemed entirely normal when viewed through a peephole, but were in fact filled with unrelated fragments of furniture and ornaments.

Young's version of the Ames Room was far more elaborate. The cross and brass candelabra appeared to stand on the altar table, but actually hung in mid-air ten feet away, suspended from the ceiling on lengths of cotton teased from his overalls. The pews had been raised on piers of prayer books and Bibles to create the illusion of an orderly nave. But once we left the projection room and entered the chapel we saw that the pews formed a stepped ramp that climbed to the ventilation grille behind the altar table. The warders glancing through the camera slit in the projection room had seen Young apparently on his knees before the cross, when in fact he had been sitting on the topmost pew in the ramp, loosening the bolts around the metal grille.

Henson was appalled by Young's escape, but I was impressed by the cleverness of this optical illusion. Like Henson, the Home Office inspectors were certain that another assassination attempt might be made on Her Majesty. However, as we gazed at that bizarre chapel something convinced me that the Queen and the President were not in danger. On the shabby wall behind the altar Young had pinned a dozen illustrations of the American and Russian space programmes, taken from newspapers and popular magazines. All the photographs of the astronauts had been defaced, the Skylab and Shuttle craft marked with obscene graffiti. He had constructed a Black Chapel, which at the same time was a complex escape device that would set him free, not merely from Daventry, but from the threat posed by the astronauts and from that far larger prison whose walls are those of space itself.

The Astro-Messiah

Colonel Thomas Jefferson Stamford, USAF (ret.). Born 1931, Brigham City, Utah. Eagle Scout, 1945. B.S. (Physics), Caltech, 1953. Graduated US Air Force Academy, 1957. Served Viet Nam, 1964–9. Enrolled NASA, 1970; deputy ground controller, Skylab III. 1974, rumoured commander of secret Apollo 20 mission to the moon which landed remote-controlled nuclear missile station in the Mare Imbrium. Retired 1975, appointed vice-president, Pepsi-Cola Corporation. 1976, script consultant to 20th Century-Fox for projected biopic *Men with Fins*.

1977, associated with the Precious Light Movement, a California-based consciousness-raising group calling for legalisation of LSD. Resigned 1978, hospitalised Veterans Administration Hospital, Fresno. On discharge begins nine months retreat at Truth Mountain, Idaho, interdenominational order of lay monks. 1979, founds Spaceways, drug rehabilitation centre, Santa Monica. 1980–1, associated with Billy Graham, shares platform on revivalist missions to Europe and Australia. 1982, visits Windsor Castle with President Reagan. 1983, forms the evangelical trust COME Incorporated, tours Alabama and Mississippi as self-proclaimed 13th Disciple. 1984, visits Africa, SE Asia, intercedes Iraq/Iran conflict, addresses NATO Council of Ministers, urges development of laser weapons and neutron bomb. 1986, guest of Royal Family at Buckingham Palace, appears in Queen's Christmas TV broadcast, successfully treats Prince William, becomes confidant and spiritual adviser to Princess Diana. Named Man of the Year by *Time* magazine, profiled by *Newsweek* as "Space-Age Messiah" and "founder of first space-based religion".

Could this much-admired former astronaut, a folk hero who clearly fulfilled the role of a 1980s Lindbergh, have been the real target of the Windsor attack? Lindbergh had once hob-nobbed with kings and chancellors, but his cranky political beliefs had become tainted by pro-Nazi sentiments. By contrast Col. Stamford's populist mix of born-again Christianity and anti-communist rhetoric seemed little more than an outsider's long shot at the White House. Now and then, watching Stamford's rallies on television, I detected the same hypertonic facial musculature that could be seen in Hitler, Qaddafi and the more excitable of Khomeini's mullahs, yet nothing worthy of the elaborate assassination attempt, a psychodrama in itself, that Matthew Young had mounted in his Lilienthal glider.

And yet . . . who better than a pioneer aeronaut to kill a pioneer astronaut, to turn the clock of space exploration back to zero?

10 February 1988. For the last three months an energetic search has failed to find any trace of Matthew Young. The Special Branch guard on the Queen, Prime Minister and senior cabinet members has been tightened, and several of the royals have been issued with small pistols. One hopes that they will avoid injuring themselves, or each other. Already the disguised fashion-accessory holster worn by Princess Diana has inspired a substantial copycat industry, and London is filled with young women wearing stylised codpieces (none of them realise why), like cast members from a musical version of *The Gunfight at the OK Corral*.

The Boy's former girlfriends and surviving relatives, his probation officer and fellow programmers at Virgin Records have been watched and/or interrogated. A few suspected sightings have occurred: in November an eccentric young man in the leather gaiters and antique costume of a World War 1 aviator enrolled for a course of lessons at Elstree Flying School, only to suffer an epileptic seizure after the first take-off. Hundreds of London Underground posters advertising Col. Stamford's Easter rally at Earls Court have been systematically defaced. At Pinewood Studios an arsonist has partially destroyed the sets for the $100 million budget science-fiction films *The Revenge of R2D2* and *C3PO Meets E.T.* A night intruder penetrated the offices of COME Inc. in the Tottenham Court Road and secretly dubbed an obscene message over Col. Stamford's inspirational address on the thousands of promotional videos. In several Piccadilly amusement arcades the Space Invaders games have been reprogrammed to present Col. Stamford's face as the target.

More significant, perhaps, a caller with the same voiceprint as Matthew Young has persistently tried to telephone the Archbishop of Canterbury. Three days ago the vergers at Westminster Abbey briefly apprehended a youth praying before a bizarre tableau consisting of Col. Stamford's blood-stained space-suit and helmet, stolen from their display case in the Science Museum, which he had set up in a niche behind the High Altar. The rare blood group, BRh, is not Col. Stamford's but The Boy's.

The reports of Matthew Young at prayer reminded me of Governor Henson's description of the prisoner seen on his knees in that illusionist chapel he had constructed at Daventry. There is an eerie contrast between the vast revivalist rally being televised at this moment from the Parc des Princes in Paris, dominated by the spotlit figure of the former astronaut, and the darkened nave of the Abbey where an escaped mental patient prayed over a stolen space-suit smeared with his own blood. The image of outer space, from which Col. Stamford draws so much of his religious inspiration, for Matthew Young seems identified with some unspecified evil, with the worship of a false messiah. His prayers in the Daventry chapel, as he knelt before the illusion of an altar, were a series of postural codes, a contortionist's attempt to free himself from Col. Stamford's sinister embrace.

I read once again the testimony collected by the Special Branch:

Margaret Downs, systems analyst, Wang Computers: "He was always praying, forever on his confounded knees. He even made me take a video of him, and studied it for hours. It was just too much . . ."

Doreen Jessel, health gym instructress: "At first I thought he was heavily into anaerobics. Some kind of dynamic meditation, he called it, all acrobatic contortions. I tried to get him to see a physiotherapist . . ."

John Hatton, probation officer: "There was a therapeutic aspect, of which he convinced me against my better judgement. The contortions seemed to mimic his epilepsy . . ."

Reverend Morgan Evans, Samaritans: "He accepted Robert Graves's notion of the club-footed messiah – that peculiar stepped gait common to various forms of religious dance and to all myths involving the Achilles tendon. He told me that it was based on the crabbed moon-walk adopted by the astronauts to cope with zero gravity . . ."

[59]

Sergeant J. Mellors, RAF Regiment: "The position was that of a kneeling marksman required to get off a series of shots with a bolt-action rifle, such as the Lee-Enfield or the Mannlicher-Carcano. I banned him from the firing range . . ."

Was Matthew Young dismantling and reassembling the elements of his own mind as if they were the constituents of an Ames Room? The pilot of the Home Office helicopter spoke graphically of the spatial disorientation felt by some of the special category prisoners being moved on the Daventry shuttle, in particular the cries and contortions of a Palestinian hijacker who imagined he was a dying astronaut. Defects of the vestibular apparatus of the ear are commonly found in hijackers (as in some shamans), the same sense of spatial disorientation that can be induced in astronauts by the high-speed turntable or the zero gravity of orbital flights.

It may be, therefore, that defects of the vestibular apparatus draw their sufferers towards high-speed aircraft, and the hijack is an unconscious attempt to cure this organic affliction. Prayer, vestibular defects, hijacking – watching Col. Stamford in the Parc des Princes, I notice that he sometimes stumbles as he bows over his lectern, his hands clasped in prayer in that characteristic spasm so familiar from the newsreels and now even mimicked by TV comedians.

Is Col. Stamford trying to hijack the world?

28 March 1988. Events are moving on apace. Colonel Thomas Jefferson Stamford has arrived in London, after completing his triumphal tour of the non-communist world. He has conferred with generals and right-wing churchmen, and calmed battlefields from the Golan Heights to the western Sahara. As always, he urges the combatants to join forces against the real enemy, pushing an anti-Soviet, church-militant line that makes the CIA look like the Red Cross. Television and newspapers show him mingling with heads of state and retired premiers, with Kohl, Thatcher and Mitterrand, with Scandinavian royals and the British monarch.

Throughout, Col. Stamford's earlier career as an astronaut is never forgotten. At his rallies in the Parc des Princes and Munich's Olympic Stadium these great arenas are transformed into what seems to be the interior of a gigantic star-ship. By the cunning use of a circular film screen, Col. Stamford's arrival at the podium is presented as a landing from outer space, to deafening extracts from *Thus Spake Zarathustra* and Holst's *Planets*. With its illusionist back-projection and trick lighting the rally becomes a huge Ames Room, a potent mix of evangelical Christianity, astronautics and cybernetic movie-making. We are in the presence of an Intelsat messiah, a mana-personality for the age of cable TV.

His thousands of followers sway in their seats, clutching COME Inc.'s promotional videos like Mao's Red Guards with their little red books. Are we seeing the first video religion, an extravagant light show with laser graphics by Lucasfilms? The message of the rallies, as of the videos, is that Col. Thomas Stamford has returned to earth to lead a moral crusade against atheistic Marxism, a Second Coming that has launched the 13th Disciple down the aisles of space from the altar of the Mare Imbrium.

Already two former Apollo astronauts have joined this crusade, resigning their directorships of Avis and Disney Corporation, and members of the Skylab and Shuttle missions have pledged their support. Will NASA one day evolve into a religious organisation? Caucus leaders in the Democratic and Republican Parties have urged Col. Stamford to stand for President. But I suspect that the Great Mission Controller in the Sky intends to bypass the Presidency and appeal directly to the US public as an astro-messiah, a space ayatollah descending to earth to set up his religious republic.

The First Church of the Divine Astronaut

These messianic strains reminded me of The Boy, the self-sworn enemy of all astronauts. On the day after the Colonel's arrival in London for the Easter rally, to be attended by Prince Charles, Princess Diana and the miraculously cured Prince William, I drove to the lock-up garage in Highbury. I had repeatedly warned the Home Office of a probable assassination attempt, but they seemed too

[61]

mesmerised by the Stamford fever that had seized the whole of London to believe that anyone would attack him.

As Constable Willings waited in the rain I stared down at the oil-stained camp bed and the sink with its empty cans of instant coffee. The Special Branch investigators had stripped the shabby garage, yet pinned to the cement wall above the bed was a postcard that they had inexplicably missed. Stepping closer, I saw that it was a reproduction of a small Samuel Palmer, "A Dream of Death by Fire", a visionary scene of the destruction of a false church by the surrounding light of a true nature. The painting had been identified by Keating as one of his most ambitious frauds.

A fake Keating to describe the death of a fake messiah? Pinned to the damp cement within the past few days, the postcard was clearly Matthew Young's invitation to me. But where would I find him? Then, through the open doors, I saw the disused Baptist church behind the row of garages.

As soon as I entered its gloomy nave I was certain that Matthew Young's target had been neither President Reagan nor the Queen. The bolt cutters borrowed from Constable Willings snapped the links of the rusting chain. When he had driven away I pushed back the worm-riddled doors. At some time in the past a television company had used the deconsecrated church to store its unwanted props. Stage sets and painted panels from a discontinued science-fiction series leaned against the walls in a dusty jumble.

I entered the aisle and stood between the pews. Then, as I stepped forward, I saw a sudden diorama of the lunar surface. In front of me was a miniature film set constructed from old *Star Wars* posters and props from *Dr Who*. Above the lunar landscape hung the figure of an astronaut flying with arms outstretched.

As I guessed, this diorama formed part of yet another Ames Room. The astronaut's figure created its illusion only when seen from the doors of the church. As I approached, however, its elements moved apart. A gloved hand hung alone, severed from the arm that seemed to support it. The detached thorax and sections of the legs drifted away from one another, suspended on threads of wire from the rafters above the nave. The head and helmet had been sliced from the shoulders, and had taken off on a flight of their own. As I stood by the altar the dismembered astronaut flew above me, like a chromium corpse blown apart by a booby-trap hidden in its life-support system.

Lying on the stone floor below this eerie spectacle was Matthew Young. He rested on his back in a scuffle of dust and cracked flagstones, his scarred mouth drawn back in a bloodless grimace to reveal the broken teeth whose caps he had crushed. He had fallen to the floor during his *grand mal* attack, and his outstretched fingers had torn a section of a *Star Wars* poster, which lay across him like a shroud. Blood pooled in a massive haematoma below his cheekbone, as if during the focal seizure of his right hand he had been trying to put out the eye with the telescopic sight of the marksman's rifle that he clasped in his fist.

I freed his tongue and windpipe, massaged his diaphragm until his breath was even, and placed a choir cushion below his shoulders. On the floor beside him were the barrel, receiver, breech and magazine of a stockless rifle whose parts he had been oiling in the moments before his attack, and which I knew he would reassemble the instant he awoke.

Easter Day, 1988. This evening Col. Stamford's rally will be held at Earls Court. Since his arrival in London, as a guest of Buckingham Palace, the former astronaut has been intensely busy, preparing that springboard which will propel him across the Atlantic. Three days ago he addressed the joint Houses of Parliament in Westminster Hall. In his televised speech he called for a crusade against the evil empire of the non-Christian world, for the construction of orbital nuclear bomb platforms, for the launching of geosynchronous laser weapons trained upon Teheran, Moscow and Peking. He seems to be demanding the destruction not merely of the Soviet Union but of the non-Christian world, the re-conquest of Jerusalem and the conversion of Islam.

It is clear that Col. Stamford is as demented as Hitler, but fortunately his last splashdown is at hand. I assume that Matthew Young will be attending the Earls Court rally this evening. I did not report him to the police, confident that he would recover in time to reassemble his rifle and make his way to one of the empty projection booths beneath the roof of the arena. Seeing Col. Stamford's arrival from "outer space", The Boy will watch him from the camera window, and listen to him urge his nuclear jihad against the forces of the anti-Christ. From that narrow but never more vital perspective, the sights of his rifle, Matthew Young will be ready once again to dismantle an illusionist space and celebrate the enduring mysteries of the Ames Room.

(1984)

Love in a Colder Climate

Anyone reading this confession in 1989, the year when I was born, would have been amazed to find me complaining about a state of affairs that must in every respect have resembled paradise. However, yesterday's heaven all too easily becomes today's hell. The greatest voluptuary dream of mankind, which has lifted the spirits of poets and painters, presidents and peasants, has turned only twenty-two years later into a living nightmare. For young men of my own genera-tion (the word provokes a shudder in the heart, if nowhere else), the situation has become so desperate that any escape seems justified. The price that I have paid for my freedom may seem excessive, but I am happy to have made this savage, if curious, bargain.

Soon after I reached my twenty-first birthday I was ordered to enlist for my two years of national service, and I remember thinking how much my father and grandfather would have envied me. On a pleasant summer evening in 2010, after a tiring day at the medical school, I was ringing the doorbell of an apartment owned by an attractive young woman whose name I had been given. I had never met her, but I was confident that she would greet me in the friendliest way – so friendly that within a few minutes we would be lying naked together in bed. Needless to say, no money would change hands, and neither she nor I would play our parts for less than the most patriotic motives. Yet both of us would loathe the sight and touch of the other and would be only too relieved when we parted an hour later.

Sure enough, the door opened to reveal a confident young bru-nette with a welcoming, if brave, smile. According to my assignment card, she was Victoria Hale, a financial journalist on a weekly news magazine. Her eyes glanced at my face and costume in the shrewd way she might have scanned a worthy but dull company prospectus.

"David Bradley?" She read my name from her own assignment card, trying hard to muster a show of enthusiasm. "You're a medical student . . . How fascinating."

"It's wonderful to meet you, Victoria," I riposted. "I've always wanted to know about . . . financial journalism."

I stood awkwardly in the centre of her apartment, my legs turning to lead. These lines of dialogue, like those that followed, had seemed preposterous when I first uttered them. But my supervisor had wisely insisted that I stick to the script, and already, after only three months of national service, I was aware that the formalised dialogue, like our absurd costumes, provided a screen behind which we could hide our real feelings.

I was wearing the standard-issue Prince Valiant suit, which a careful survey of the TV programmes of the 1960s had confirmed to be the most sexually attractive costume for the predatory male. In a suit like this Elvis Presley had roused the Las Vegas matrons to an ecstasy of abandon, though I found its tassels, gold braid and tight crotch as comfortable as the decorations on a Christmas tree.

Victoria Hale, for her part, was wearing a classic Playboy bunny outfit of the same period. As she served me a minute measure of vodka her breasts managed to be both concealed and exposed in a way that an earlier generation must have found irresistibly fascinating, like the rabbit tail that bounced above her contorted buttocks, a furry metronome which already had me glancing at my wristwatch.

"Mr Bradley, we can get it over with now," she remarked briskly. She had departed from the script but quickly added: "Now tell me about your work, David. I can see that you're such an interesting man."

She was as bored with me as I was uneasy with her, but in a few minutes we would be lying together in bed. With luck my hormonal and nervous systems would come to my rescue and bring our meeting to a climax. We would initial each other's assignment cards and make a thankful return to our ordinary lives. Yet the very next evening another young man in a Prince Valiant suit would ring the doorbell of the apartment, and this thoughtful journalist would greet him in her grotesque costume. And I, in turn, at eight o'clock would put aside my anatomy textbooks and set out through the weary streets to an arranged meeting in an unknown apartment, where some pleasant young woman – student, waitress or librarian – would welcome me with the same formal smile and stoically take me to bed.

To understand this strange world where sex has become compulsory, one must look back to the ravages brought about in the last decade of the 20th century by the scourge of AIDS and the pandemic of associated diseases clustered around its endlessly mutating virus. By the mid-1990s this ferocious plague had begun to threaten more than the millions of individual lives. The institutions of marriage and the family, ideals of parenthood, and the social contract between the sexes, even the physical relationship between man and woman, had been corrupted by this cruel disease. Terrified of infection, people learnt to abstain from every kind of physical or sexual contact. From puberty onward, an almost visible cordon divided the sexes. In offices, factories, schools and universities the young men and women kept their distance. My own parents in the 1980s were among the last generation to marry without any fear of what their union might produce. By the 1990s, too often, courtship and marriage would be followed by a series of mysterious ailments, anxious visits to a test clinic, a positive diagnosis and the terminal hospice.

Faced with a plunging birth rate and with a nation composed almost entirely of solitary celibates, the government could resort only to its traditional instruments – legislation and compulsion. Urged on by the full authority of the Protestant and Catholic churches, the Third Millennium was greeted with the momentous announcement that thenceforth sex would be compulsory. All fertile, healthy and HIV-negative young men and women were required to register for their patriotic duty. On reaching their twenty-first birthdays they were assigned a personal supervisor (usually a local clergyman, the priesthood alone having the moral qualifications for such a delicate task), who drew up a list of possible mates and arranged a programme of sexual liaisons. Within a year, it was hoped, the birth rate would soar, and marriage and the family would be re-established.

At first, only one assignation each week was required, but the birth rate stubbornly refused to respond, possibly as a result of the sexual ineptness of these celibate young men and women. By the year 2005 the number of compulsory assignations was raised to three each week. Since clearly nothing could be left to nature, the participants were issued with costumes designed to enhance their attractiveness. In addition to the Prince Valiant and the Bunny Girl, there were the Castilian Waiter and the Gypsy Brigand for men and the Cheerleader and the Miss America swimsuit for women.

Even so, the earliest participants would often sit tongue-tied for hours, unable to approach each other, let alone hold hands. From then on they were carefully coached in the amatory arts by their clergymen-supervisors, who would screen erotic videos for the young recruits in their church halls, by now substantial warehouses of pornographic films and magazines.

As could be expected, the threat of two years of enforced sexual activity was deeply resented by the conscripted young men and women. Draft-dodging was carried to extreme lengths, of which vasectomy was the most popular, any perpetrators being sentenced to a testicular transplant. To prevent the young people from failing to perform their sexual duties, a network of undercover inspectors (usually novice priests and nuns, since only they possessed the necessary spirit of self-sacrifice) posed as the participants and would exact fierce on-the-spot fines for any slackening-off or lack of zeal.

All this at last had its effect on the birth rate, which began its reluctant ascent. The news was little consolation to those like myself, who every evening were obliged to leave our homes and trudge the streets on the way to yet another hour of loveless sex. How I longed for June 2012, when I would complete my period of patriotic duty and begin my real sex life of eternal celibacy.

Those dreams, though, came to an abrupt end in the spring of 2011, when I called upon Lucille McCabe. After meeting her I woke to discover a lost world of passion and the affections whose existence I had never suspected, and to fulfill my life's ambition in a way I had not foreseen.

Lucille McCabe, my assignment for the evening, lived in the

Spanish quarter of the city, and to avoid any catcalls – those of us doing our patriotic duty were figures of fun, not envy – I had dressed in my Castilian Waiter costume. The apartment was in a nondescript building kept on its feet by an armature of crumbling fire escapes. An elevator surely booked into a museum of industrial archaeology carried me grudgingly to the seventh floor. The bell hung by a single exposed wire, and I had to tap several times on the door. The silence made me hope that Miss McCabe, a lecturer in English literature, had been called away for the evening.

But the door opened with a jerk, revealing a small, white-faced young woman with spiky black hair, dressed in a polka-dot leotard like a punk circus clown.

"Miss McCabe . . . ?" I began. "Are you – "

"Ready to order?" She gazed with mock wide eyes at my waiter's costume. "Yes, I'll have a paella with a side dish of gambas. And don't forget the Tabasco."

"Tabasco? Look, I'm David Bradley, your partner for – "

"Relax, Mr Bradley." She closed the door and snatched the keys from the lock, which she jingled in my face. "It was a joke. Remember those?"

"Only just." Clearly I was in the presence of a maverick, one of those wayward young women who affected an antic air as a way of rising above the occasion. "Well, it's wonderful to see you, Lucille. I've always wanted to know about English literature."

"Forget it. How long have you been doing this? You don't look totally numbed." She stood with her back to me by the crowded bookshelf, fingers drumming along the titles as if hunting for some manual that would provide a solution to the problem posed by my arrival. For all the bravado, her shoulders were shaking. "Is this where I fix you a drink? I can't remember that awful script."

"Skip the drink. We can get straight on with it if you're in a hurry."

"I'm not in a hurry at all." She walked stiffly into the bedroom and sat like a moody teenager on the unmade divan. Nothing in my counselling sessions, the long hours watching porno videos in the church hall, had prepared me for all this – the non-regulation costume, the tousled sheets, the absence of flattering chitchat. Was she a new kind of undercover inspector, an *agent provocateur* targeted at those potential subversives like myself? Already I saw my work norm increased to seven evenings a week. Beyond that lay the fearsome threat of a testicular booster . . .

Then I noticed her torn assignment card on the carpet at her feet. No inspector, however devious, would ever maltreat an assignment card.

Wondering how to console her, I stepped forward. But as I crossed the threshold a small, strong hand shot up.

"Stay there!" She gazed at me with the desperate look of a child about to be assaulted, and I realised that for all her fierceness she was a novice recruit, probably on her first assignment. The spiked tips of her hair were trembling like the eye feathers of a trapped peafowl.

"All right, you can come in. Do you want something to eat? I can guarantee the best scrambled egg in town, my hands are shaking so much. How do you put up with all this?"

"I don't think about it any more."

"I don't think about anything else. Look, Mr Bradley – David, or whatever you're called – I can't go through with this. I don't want to fight with you . . ."

"Don't worry." I raised my hands, already thinking about the now free evening. "I'm on my way. The rules forbid all use of force, no fumbling hands or wrestling."

"How sensible. And how different from my grandmother's day." She smiled bleakly, as if visualising the courtship that had led to the conception of her own mother. With a nervous shrug, she followed me to the door. "Tell me, what happens next? I know you have to report me."

"Well . . . there's nothing too serious." I hesitated to describe the long counselling sessions that lay ahead, the weeks of being harangued by relays of nuns brandishing their videos. After all the talk there was chemotherapy, when she would be so sedated that nothing mattered, and she would close her eyes and think of her patriotic duty and the next generation, the playgrounds full of laughing tots, one of them her own . . . "I shouldn't worry. They're very civilised. At least you'll get a better apartment."

"Oh, thanks. Once, you must have been rather sweet. But they get you in the end . . ."

I took the latchkey from her hand, wondering how to reassure her. The dye had run down her powdered forehead, a battle line re-drawn across her brain. She stood with her back against the bookshelves, a woad-streaked Boadicea facing the Roman legions. Despite her distress, I had the curious sense that she was as con-cerned for me as for herself and even now was trying to work out some strategy that would save us both.

"No..." I closed the door and locked it again. "They won't get you. Not necessarily..."

My love affair with Lucille McCabe began that evening, but the details of our life together belong to the private domain. Not that there is anything salacious to reveal. As it happens, our relationship was never consummated in the physical sense, but this did not in any way diminish my deep infatuation with this remarkable young woman. The long months of my national service notwithstanding, the hundreds of reluctant Rebeccas and stoical Susans, I soon felt that Lucille McCabe was the only woman I had ever really known. During the six months of our clandestine affair I discovered a wealth of emotion and affection that made me envy all earlier generations.

At the start, my only aim was to save Lucille. I forged signatures, hoodwinked a distracted supervisor confused by the derelict apart-ment building, begged or bribed my friends to swap shifts, and Lucille feigned a pregnancy with the aid of a venal laboratory techni-cian. Marriage or any monogamous relationship was taboo during the period of one's patriotic duty, the desired aim being an open promiscuity and the greatest possible stirring of the gene pool. Nonetheless, I was able to spend almost all my spare time with Lucille, acting as lover, night watchman, spymaster and bodyguard. She, in turn, made sure that my medical studies were not neglected. Once I had qualified and she herself was free to marry, we would legally become man and wife.

Inevitably we were discovered by a suspicious supervisor with an over-sensitive computer. I had already realised that we would be exposed, and during these last months I became more and more pro-tective of Lucille, even feeling the first pangs of jealousy. I would attend her lectures, sitting in the back row and resenting any student who asked an over-elaborate question. At my insistence she abandoned her punk hairstyle for something less provocative and modestly lowered her eyes whenever a man passed her in the street.

All this tension was to explode when the supervisor arrived at Lucille's apartment. The sight of this dark-eyed young Jesuit in his Gypsy Brigand costume, mouthing his smooth amatory patter as he expertly steered Lucille toward her bedroom, proved too much for me. I gave way to a paroxysm of violence, hurling the fellow from the apartment.

From the moment the ambulance and police were called, our scheme was over. Lucille was assigned to a rehabilitation centre, once a church home for fallen mothers, and I was brought before a national service tribunal.

In vain I protested that I wished to marry Lucille and father her child. I had merely behaved like a male of old and was passionately dedicated to my future wife and family.

But this, I was told, was a selfish aberration. I was found guilty of the romantic fallacy and convicted of having an exalted and idealised vision of woman. I was sentenced to a further three years of patriotic duty.

If I rejected this, I would face the ultimate sanction.

Aware that by choosing the latter I would be able to see Lucille, I made my decision. The tribunal despaired of me, but as a generous concession to a former student of medicine, they allowed me to select my own surgeon.

(1989)

The Largest Theme Park
in the World

The creation of a united Europe, so long desired and so bitterly
contested, had certain unexpected consequences. The fulfilment of
this age-old dream was a cause of justified celebration, of countless
street festivals, banquets and speeches of self-congratulation. But
the Europe which had given birth to the Renaissance and the Protestant Reformation, to modern science and the industrial revolution,
had one last surprise up its sleeve.

Needless to say, nothing of this was apparent in 1993. The demolition of so many fiscal and bureaucratic barriers to trade led directly
to the goal of a Europe at last united in a political and cultural federation. In 1995, the headiest year since 1968, the necessary legislation
was swiftly passed by a dozen parliaments, which dissolved themselves and assigned their powers to the European Assembly at
Strasbourg. So there came into being the new Europe, a visionary
realm that would miraculously fuse the spirits of Charlemagne
and the smart card, Michelangelo and Club Med, St Augustine and
St-Laurent.

Happily exhausted by their efforts, the new Europeans took off for
the beaches of the Mediterranean, their tribal mating ground.
Blessed by a benevolent sun and a greenhouse sky, the summer of
1995 ran from April to October. A hundred million Europeans
basked on the sand, leaving behind little more than an army of care-
takers to supervise the museums, galleries and cathedrals. Excited by
the idea of a federal Europe, a vast influx of tourists arrived from the
United States, Japan and the newly liberated nations of the Soviet
bloc. Guide-books in hand, they gorged themselves on the culture

and history of Europe, which had now achieved its spiritual destiny of becoming the largest theme park in the world.

Sustained by these tourist revenues, the ecu soared above the dollar and yen, even though offices and factories remained deserted from Athens to the Atlantic. Indeed, it was only in the autumn of 1995 that the economists at Brussels resigned themselves to the paradox which no previous government had accepted – contrary to the Protestant ethic, which had failed so lamentably in the past, the less that Europe worked the more prosperous and contented it became. Delighted to prove this point, the millions of vacationing Europeans on the beaches of the Mediterranean scarcely stirred from their sun-mattresses. Autoroutes and motorways were silent, and graphs of industrial production remained as flat as the cerebral functions of the brain-dead.

An even more significant fact soon emerged. Most of the vacationing Europeans had extended their holidays from two to three months, but a substantial minority had decided not to return at all. Along the beaches of the Costa del Sol and Côte d'Azur, thousands of French, British and German tourists failed to catch their return flights from the nearby airport. Instead, they remained in their hotels and apartments, lay beside their swimming pools and dedicated themselves to the worship of their own skins.

At first this decision to stay was largely confined to the young and unmarried, to former students and the traditional lumpen-intelligentsia of the beach. But these latter-day refuseniks soon included lawyers, doctors and accountants. Even families with children chose to remain on perpetual holiday. Ignoring the telegrams and phone calls from their anxious employers in Amsterdam, Paris and Düsseldorf, they made polite excuses, applied sun oil to their shoulders and returned to their sail-boats and pedalos. It became all too clear that in rejecting the old Europe of frontiers and national self-interest they had also rejected the bourgeois values that hid behind them. A demanding occupation, a high disposable income, a future mortgaged to the gods of social and professional status, had all been abandoned.

At any event, a movement confined to a few resorts along the Mediterranean coast had, by November 1995, involved tens of thousands of holidaymakers. Those who returned home did so with mixed feelings. By the spring of 1996 more than a million expatriates had settled in permanent exile among the hotels and apartment complexes of the Mediterranean.

By summer this number vastly increased, and brought with it huge demographic and psychological changes. So far, the effects of the beach exodus on the European economy had been slight. Tourism and the sale of large sections of industry to eager Japanese corporations had kept the ecu afloat. As for the exiles in Minorca, Mykonos and the Costa Brava, the cost of living was low and basic necessities few. The hippies and ex-students turned to petty theft and slept on the beach. The lawyers and accountants were able to borrow from their banks when their own resources ran out, offering their homes and businesses as collateral. Wives sold their jewellery, and elderly relatives were badgered into small loans.

Fortunately, the sun continued to shine through the numerous ozone windows and the hottest summer of the century was widely forecast. The determination of the exiles never to return to their offices and factories was underpinned by a new philosophy of leisure and a sense of what constituted a worthwhile life. The logic of the annual beach holiday, which had sustained Europe since the Second World War, had merely been taken to its conclusion. Crime and delinquency were non-existent and the social and racial tolerance of those reclining in adjacent poolside chairs was virtually infinite.

Was Europe about to lead the world in another breakthrough for the third millennium? A relaxed and unpuritan sexual regime now flourished and there was a new-found pride in physical excellence. A host of sporting activities took place, there were classes in judo and karate, aerobics and tai-chi. The variety of fringe philosophies began to rival those of California. The first solar cults emerged on the beaches of Torremolinos and St Tropez. Where once the Mediterranean coast had been Europe's Florida, a bland parade of marinas and hotels, it was now set to be its Venice Beach, a hot-house of muscle-building and millennial dreams.

In the summer of 1996 the first challenge occurred to this regime of leisure. By now the beach communities comprised some five million exiles, and their financial resources were exhausted. Credit cards had long been cancelled, bank accounts frozen, and governments in Paris, London and Bonn waited for the return of the expatriates to their desks and work-benches.

Surprisingly, the determination of the beach communities never wavered. Far from catching their long-delayed return flights, the exiles decided to hold on to their place in the sun. Soon this brought them into direct conflict with local hoteliers and apartment owners, who found themselves housing a huge population of non-paying guests. The police were called in, and the first open riots occurred on the beaches of Malaga, Menton and Rimini.

The exiles, however, were difficult to dislodge. A year of sun and exercise had turned them into a corps of superb athletes, for whom the local shopkeepers, waiters and hoteliers were no match. Gangs of muscular young women, expert in the martial arts, roamed the supermarkets of Spain and the Côte d'Azur, fearlessly helping themselves from the shelves. Acts of open intimidation quickly subdued the managers of hotels and apartment houses.

Local police chiefs, for their part, were reluctant to intervene, for fear of damaging the imminent summer tourist trade. The lawyers and accountants among the exiles, all far more educated and intelligent than their provincial rivals, were adept at challenging any eviction orders or charges of theft. The once passive regime of sun and sand had given way to a more militant mood, sustained by the exiles' conviction in the moral and spiritual rightness of their cause. Acting together, they commandeered any empty villas or apartment houses, whose owners were either too terrified to protest or fled the scene altogether.

The cult of physical perfection had gripped everyone's imagination. Bodies deformed by years bent over the word-processor and fast-food counter were now slim and upright, as ideally proportioned as the figures on the Parthenon frieze. The new evangelism concealed behind the exercise and fitness fads of the 1980s now reappeared. A devotion to physical perfection ruled their lives more strictly than any industrial taskmaster.

Out of necessity, leisure had moved into a more disciplined phase. At dawn the resort beaches of the Mediterranean were filled with companies of martial art enthusiasts, kicking and grunting in unison. Brigades of handsomely tanned men and women drilled together as they faced the sun. No longer did they devote their spare time to lying on the sand, but to competitive sports and fiercely contested track events.

Already the first community leaders had emerged from the strongest and most charismatic of the men and women. The casual anarchy of the earliest days had given way to a sensible and co-operative democracy, where members of informal beach groups had voted on their best course of action before seizing an empty hotel or raiding a wine-store. But this democratic phase had failed to meet the needs and emotions of the hour, and the beach communities soon evolved into more authoritarian form.

The 1996 holiday season brought a welcome respite and millions of new recruits, whose purses were bulging with ecus. When they arrived at Marbella, Ibiza, La Grande Motte and Sestri Levante they found themselves eagerly invited to join the new beach communities. By August 1996, when almost the whole of Europe had set off for the coasts of the sun, the governments of its member countries were faced with the real possibility that much of their populations would not return. Not only would offices and factories be closed forever, but there would be no one left to man the museums and galleries, to collect the dollars, yen and roubles of the foreign tourists who alone sustained their economies. The prospect appeared that the Louvre and Buckingham Palace might be sold to a Japanese hotel corporation, that Chartres and Cologne cathedrals would become subsidiaries of the Disney company.

Forced to act, the Strasbourg Assembly dispatched a number of task forces to the south. Posing as holidaymakers, teams of investigators roamed the cafés and swimming pools. But the pathetic attempts of these bikini bureaucrats to infiltrate and destabilise the beach enclaves came to nothing, and many defected to the ranks of the exiles.

So at last, in October 1996, the Strasbourg Assembly announced that the beaches of the Mediterranean were closed, that all forms of exercise outside the workplace or the bedroom were illegal, and that the suntan was a prohibited skin embellishment. Lastly, the

Assembly ordered its 30 million absent citizens to return home.

Needless to say, these commands were ignored. The beach people who occupied the linear city of the Mediterranean coast, some 3,000 miles long and 300 metres wide, were now a very different breed. The police and gendarmerie who arrived at the coastal resorts found militant bands of body-worshippers who had no intention of resuming their previous lives.

Aware that a clash with the authorities would take place, they had begun to defend their territory, blockading the beach roads with abandoned cars, fortifying the entrances to hotels and apartment houses. By day their scuba teams hunted the coastal waters for fish, while at night raiding parties moved inland, stealing sheep and looting the fields of their vegetable crops. Large sections of Malaga, St Tropez and Corfu were now occupied by exiles, while many of the smaller resorts such as Rosas and Formentera were wholly under their control.

The first open conflict, at Golfe-Juan, was typically short-lived and indecisive. Perhaps unconsciously expecting the Emperor to come ashore, as he had done after his escape from Elba, the police were unable to cope with the militant brigade of bronzed and naked mothers, chanting green and feminist slogans, who advanced towards their water-cannon. Commandos of dentists and architects, releasing their fiercest karate kicks, strutted through the narrow streets in what seemed to be a display of a new folk tradition, attracting unmanageable crowds of American and Japanese tourists from their Cannes hotels. At Port-Vendres, Sitges, Bari and Fréjus the police fell back in confusion, unable to distinguish between the exiles and authentic visiting holidaymakers.

When the police returned in force, supported by units of the army, their arrival only increased the determination of the beach people. The polyglot flavour of the original settlers had given way to a series of national groups recruiting their members from their traditional resorts – the British at Torremolinos, Germans at Rosas, French at Juan les Pins. The resistance within these enclaves reflected their national identity – a rabble of drunken British hooligans roamed the streets of Torremolinos, exposing their fearsome buttocks to the riot police. The Germans devoted themselves to hard work and duty, erecting a Siegfried Line of sand bunkers around the beaches of Rosas, while the massed nipples of Juan were more than enough to hopelessly dazzle the gendarmerie.

In return, each of these national enclaves produced its characteristic leaders. The British resorts were dominated by any number of would-be Thatchers, fierce ladies in one-piece bathing suits who invoked the memory of Churchill and proclaimed their determination to "fight them on the beaches and never, *never* surrender". Gaullist throwbacks spoke loftily of the grandeur of French sun and sand, while the Italians proclaimed their "mare nostrum".

But above all the tone of these beach-führers was uniformly authoritarian. The sometime holiday exiles now enjoyed lives of fierce self-discipline coupled with a mystical belief in the powers of physical strength. Athletic prowess was admired above all, a cult of bodily perfection mediated through group gymnastic displays on the beaches, quasi-fascistic rallies, in which thousands of well-drilled participants slashed the dawn air with their karate chops and chanted in a single voice at the sun. These bronzed and handsome figures with their thoughtless sexuality looked down on their tourist compatriots with a sense of almost racial superiority.

It was clear that Europe, where so much of Western civilisation had originated, had given birth to yet another significant trend, the first totalitarian system based on leisure. From the sun-lounge and the swimming pool, from the gymnasium and disco, had come a nationalistic and authoritarian creed with its roots in the realm of pleasure rather than that of work.

By the spring of 1997, as Brussels fumbled and Strasbourg debated, the 30 million people of the beach were beginning to look north for the first time. They listened to their leaders talking of national living space, of the hordes of alien tourists with their soulless dollars and yen, of the tired blood of their compatriots yearning to be invigorated. As they stood on the beaches of Marbella, Juan, Rimini and Naxos they swung their arms in unison, chanting their exercise songs as they heard the call to march north, expel the invading tourists and reclaim their historic heartlands.

So, in the summer of 1997 they set off along the deserted autoroutes and motorways in the greatest invasion which Europe has ever known, intent on seizing their former homes, determined to reinstate a forgotten Europe of nations, each jealous of its frontiers, happy to guard its history, tariff barriers and insularity.

(1989)

Answers to a Questionnaire

1) Yes.
2) Male (?)
3) c/o Terminal 3, London Airport, Heathrow.
4) Twenty-seven.
5) Unknown.
6) Dr Barnardo's Primary, Kingston-upon-Thames; HM Borstal, Send, Surrey; Brunel University Computer Sciences Department.
7) Floor cleaner, Mecca Amusement Arcades, Leicester Square.
8) If I can avoid it.
9) Systems Analyst, Sperry-Univac, 1979–83.
10) Manchester Crown Court, 1984.
11) Credit card and computer fraud.
12) Guilty.
13) Two years, HM Prison, Parkhurst.
14) Stockhausen, de Kooning, Jack Kerouac.
15) Whenever possible.
16) Twice a day.
17) NSU, herpes, gonorrhoea.
18) Husbands.
19) My greatest ambition is to turn into a TV programme.
20) I first saw the deceased on 17 February 1986, in the chapel at London Airport. He was praying in the front pew.
21) At the time I was living in an out-of-order cubicle in the air traffic controllers' washroom in Terminal 3.
22) Approx. 5 ft 7 in, aged thirty-three, slim build, albino skin and thin black beard, some kind of crash injuries to both hands. At first I thought he was a Palestinian terrorist.

23) He was wearing the stolen uniform trousers of an El Al flight engineer.

24) With my last money I bought him a prawnburger in the mezzanine cafeteria. He thanked me and, although not carrying a bank-card, extracted £100 from a service till on the main concourse.

25) Already I was convinced that I was in the presence of a messianic figure who would help me to penetrate the Nat West deposit account computer codes.

26) No sexual activity occurred.

27) I took him to Richmond Ice Rink where he immediately performed six triple salchows. I urged him to take up ice-dancing with an eye to the European Championships and eventual gold at Seoul, but he began to trace out huge double spirals on the ice. I tried to convince him that these did not feature in the compulsory figures, but he told me that the spirals represented a model of synthetic DNA.

28) No.

29) He gave me to understand that he had important connections at the highest levels of government.

30) Suite 17B, London Penta Hotel. I slept on the floor in the bathroom.

31) Service tills in Oxford Street, Knightsbridge and Earls Court.

32) Approx. £275,000 in three weeks.

33) Porno videos. He took a particular interest in Kamera Klimax and Electric Blue.

34) Almost every day.

35) When he was drunk. He claimed that he brought the gift of eternal life.

36) At the Penta Hotel I tried to introduce him to Torvill and Dean. He was interested in meeting only members of the Stock Exchange and Fellows of the Royal Society.

37) Females of all ages.

38) Group sex.

39) Marie Drummond, twenty-two, sales assistant, HMV Records; Denise Attwell, thirty-seven, research supervisor, Geigy Pharmaceuticals; Florence Burgess, fifty-five, deaconess, Bible

[82]

Society Bookshop; Angelina Gomez, twenty-three, air hostess, Iberian Airways; Phoebe Adams, forty-three, Cruise protestor, Camp Orange, Greenham Common.

40) Sometimes, at his suggestion.

41) Unsatisfactory.

42) Premature ejaculation; impotence.

43) He urged me to have a sex-change operation.

44) National Gallery, Wallace Collection, British Museum. He was much intrigued by representations of Jesus, Zoroaster and the Gautama Buddha, and commented on the likenesses.

45) With the permission of the manager, NE District, British Telecom.

46) We erected the antenna on the roof of the Post Office Tower.

47) 2500 KHz.

48) Towards the constellation Orion.

49) I heard his voice, apparently transmitted from the star Betelgeuse 2000 years ago.

50) Interference to TV reception all over London and the South-east.

51) No. 1 in the BARB Ratings, exceeding the combined audiences for *Coronation Street*, *Dallas* and *Dynasty*.

52) Regular visitors included Princess Diana, Prince Charles and Dr Billy Graham.

53) He hired the Wembley Conference Centre.

54) 'Immortality in the Service of Mankind'.

55) Guests were drawn from the worlds of science and politics, the church, armed forces and the Inland Revenue.

56) Generous fees.

57) Service tills in Mayfair and Regent Street.

58) He had a keen appreciation of money, but was not impressed when I told him of Torvill and Dean's earnings.

59) He was obsessed by the nature of the chemical bond.

60) Sitting beside him at the top table were: (1) The Leader of Her Majesty's Opposition, (2) The President of the Royal Society, (3) The Archbishop of Canterbury, (4) The Chief Rabbi, (5) The Chairman of the Diners Club, (6) The Chairman of the Bank of England, (7) The General Secretary of the Inland

Revenue Staff Federation, (8) The President of Hertz Rent-a-Car, (9) The President of IBM, (10) The Chief of the General Staff, (11) Dr Henry Kissinger, (12) Myself.

61) He stated that synthetic DNA introduced into the human germ plasm would arrest the process of ageing and extend human life almost indefinitely.

62) Perhaps 1 million years.

63) He announced that Princess Diana was immortal.

64) Astonishment/disbelief.

65) He advised the audience to invest heavily in leisure industries.

66) The value of the pound sterling rose to $8.75.

67) American TV networks, *Time* magazine, *Newsweek*.

68) The Second Coming.

69) He expressed strong disappointment at the negative attitude of the Third World.

70) The Kremlin.

71) He wanted me to become the warhead of a Cruise missile.

72) My growing disenchantment.

73) Sexual malaise.

74) He complained that I was spending too much time at Richmond Ice Rink.

75) The Royal Proclamation.

76) The pound sterling rose to $75.50.

77) Prince Andrew. Repeatedly.

78) Injection into the testicles.

79) The side-effects were permanent impotence and sterility. However, as immortality was ensured, no further offspring would be needed and the procreative urge would atrophy.

80) I seriously considered a sex-change operation.

81) Government White Paper on Immortality.

82) Compulsory injection into the testicles of the entire male population over eleven years.

83) Smith & Wesson short-barrel thirty-eight.

84) Entirely my own idea.

85) Many hours at Richmond Ice Rink trying unsuccessfully to erase the patterns of DNA.

86) Westminster Hall.

87) Premeditated. I questioned his real motives.
88) Assassination.
89) I was neither paid nor incited by agents of a foreign power.
90) Despair. I wish to go back to my cubicle at London Airport.
91) Between Princess Diana and the Governor of Nevada.
92) At the climax of *Thus Spake Zarathustra*.
93) Seven feet.
94) Three shots.
95) Blood Group O.
96) I did not wish to spend the rest of eternity in my own company.
97) I was visited in the death cell by the special envoy of the Archbishop of Canterbury.
98) That I had killed the Son of God.
99) He walked with a slight limp. He told me that, as a condemned prisoner, I alone had been spared the sterilising injections, and that the restoration of the national birthrate was now my sole duty.
100) Yes.

(1985)

The Air Disaster

The news that the world's largest airliner had crashed into the sea near Acapulco with a thousand passengers on board reached me while I was attending the annual film festival at the resort. When the first radio reports were relayed over the conference loudspeakers I and my fellow journalists abandoned our seats in the auditorium and hurried out into the street. Together we stared silently at the sunlit ocean, almost expecting to see an immense cascade of water rising from the distant waves.

Like everyone else, I realised that this was the greatest disaster in the history of world aviation, and a tragedy equal to the annihilation of a substantial town. I had lost all interest in the film festival, and was glad when the manager of my television station in Mexico City ordered me to drive to the scene of the accident, some thirty miles to the south.

As I set off in my car I remembered when these huge airliners had come into service. Although they represented no significant advance in aviation technology – in effect they were double-decker versions of an earlier airliner – there was something about the figure 1000 that touched the imagination, setting off all kinds of forebodings that no amount of advertising could dispel.

A thousand passengers ... I mentally counted them off – businessmen, elderly nuns, children returning to their parents, eloping lovers, diplomats, even a would-be hijacker. It was this almost perfect cross-section of humanity, like the census sample of an opinion pollster, that brought the disaster home. I found myself glancing compulsively at the sea, expecting to see the first handbags and life-jackets washed ashore on the empty beaches.

The sooner I could photograph a piece of floating debris and return to Acapulco – even to the triviality of the film festival – the happier I would feel. Unfortunately, the road was jammed with southbound traffic. Clearly every other journalist, both foreign and Mexican, present at the festival had been ordered to the scene of the disaster. Television camera-vans, police vehicles and the cars of over-eager sightseers were soon bumper to bumper. Annoyed by their ghoulish interest in the tragedy, I found myself hoping that there would be no trace of the aircraft when we arrived and stepped onto the beach.

In fact, as I listened to the radio bulletins, there was almost no information about the crash. The commentators already on the site, cruising the choppy waters of the Pacific in rented motor-boats, reported that there were no signs of any oil or wreckage.

Sadly, however, there was little doubt that the aircraft had crashed somewhere. The flight-crew of another airliner had seen the huge jet explode in mid-air, probably the victim of sabotage. Eerily, the one piece of hard information, constantly played and replayed over the radio, was the last transmission from the pilot of the huge aeroplane, reporting a fire in his cargo hold.

So the aircraft had come down – but where, exactly? For all the lack of information, the traffic continued to press southwards. Behind me, an impatient American newsreel team decided to overtake the line of crawling vehicles on the pedestrian verge, and the first altercations soon broke out. Police stood at the major crossroads, and with their usual flair managed to slow down any progress. After an hour of this, my car's engine began to boil, and I was forced to turn the lame vehicle into a roadside garage.

Sitting irritably in the forecourt, and well aware that I was unlikely to reach the crash site until the late afternoon, I looked away from the almost stationary traffic to the mountains a few miles inland. The foothills of the coastal range, they rose sharply into a hard and cloudless sky, their steep peaks lit by the sun. It occurred to me then that no one had actually witnessed the descent of the stricken airliner into the sea. Somewhere above the mountains the explosion had taken place, and the likely trajectory would have carried the unhappy machine into the Pacific. On the other hand, an observational error of a few miles, the miscalculation of a few

[87]

seconds by the flight-crew who had seen the explosion, would make possible an impact point well inland.

By coincidence, two journalists in a nearby car were discussing exactly this possibility with the garage attendant filling their fuel tank. This young man was gesturing towards the mountains, where a rough road wound up a steep valley. He slapped his hands together, as if mimicking an explosion.

The journalists watched him sceptically, unimpressed by the story and put off by the young man's rough appearance and almost unintelligible local dialect. Paying him off, they turned their car onto the road and rejoined the slowly moving caravan to the south.

The attendant watched them go, his mind on other things. When he had filled my radiator, I asked him:

"You saw an explosion in the mountains?"

"I might have done – it's hard to say. It could have been lightning or a snow-slide."

"You didn't see the aircraft?"

"No – I can't say that."

He shrugged, only interested in going off duty. I waited while he handed over to his relief, climbed onto the back of a friend's motor-cycle and set off along the coast with everyone else.

I looked up at the road into the valley. By luck, the farm track behind the garage joined it 400 yards inland on the far side of a field.

Ten minutes later I was driving up the valley and away from the coastal plain. What made me follow this hunch that the aircraft had come down in the mountains? Self-interest, clearly, the hope of scooping all my colleagues and at last impressing my editor. Ahead of me was a small village, a run-down collection of houses grouped around two sides of a sloping square. Half a dozen farmers sat outside the tavern, little more than a window in a stone wall. Already the coast road was far below, part of another world. From this height someone would certainly have noticed the explosion if the aircraft had fallen here. I would question a few people; if they had seen nothing I would turn round and head south with everyone else.

As I entered the village I remembered how poverty-stricken this area of Mexico had always been, almost unchanged since the early 19th century. Most of the modest stone houses were still without electricity. There was a single television aerial, and a few elderly cars, wrecks on wheels, sat on the roadside among pieces of rusting agricultural equipment. The worn hill-slopes stretched up the valley, and the dull soil had long since given up its meagre fertility.

However, the chance remained that these villagers had seen something, a flash, perhaps, or even a sight of the stricken airliner plummeting overhead towards the sea.

I stopped my car in the cobbled square and walked across to the farmers outside the tavern.

"I'm looking for the crashed aircraft," I told them. "It may have come down near here. Have any of you seen anything?"

They were staring at my car, clearly a far more glamorous machine than anything that might fall from the sky. They shook their heads, waving their hands in a peculiarly secretive way. I knew that I had wasted my time in setting out on this private expedition. The mountains rose around me on all sides, the valleys dividing like the entrances to an immense maze.

As I turned to go back to my car one of the older farmers touched my arm. He pointed casually to a narrow valley sheltering between two adjacent peaks high above us.

"The aircraft?" I repeated.

"It's up there."

"What? Are you sure?" I tried to control my excitement for fear of giving anything away.

The old man nodded, his interest fading. "Yes. At the end of that valley. It's a long way."

Within moments I had set off again, restraining myself with difficulty from over-taxing the engine. The few vague words of this old man convinced me that I was on the right track and about to achieve the scoop I had yearned for throughout my professional career. However casually he had spoken he had meant what he said.

I pressed on up the narrow road, forcing the car in and out of the pot-holes and rain-gullies. At each turn of the road I half-expected to see the tail-plane of the aircraft poised on a distant crag, and the hundreds of bodies scattered down the mountain slopes like a fallen army. I started to run over in my mind the opening paragraphs of my dispatch, telephoned to my startled editor while my rivals were fifty miles away staring into the empty sea. It was vital to achieve the right marriage of sensation and compassion, that irresistible combination of ruthless realism and melancholy invocation. I would describe the first ominous discovery of a single aircraft seat on a hillside, a poignant trail of ruptured suitcases, a child's fluffy toy and then – a valley floor covered with corpses.

For an hour I pressed on up the road, now and then having to stop and kick away the boulders that blocked my path. This remote infertile region was almost deserted. At intervals an isolated hovel clung to a hillside, a section of telegraph wire followed me overhead for half a mile before ending abruptly, as if the telephone company years beforehand had realised that there was no one here to make or receive a call.

Once again, I began to have second thoughts. Had the old villager been playing me along? Surely if he had seen the aircraft come down he would have been more concerned?

The coastal plain and the sea were now miles behind me, visible only for brief moments as I followed the broken road up the valley. Looking back at the sunlit coast through the rear mirror, I carelessly rolled the car over some heavy rubble. After the collision underneath I could tell from the different note of the exhaust that I had damaged the muffler.

Cursing myself for having embarked on this lunatic chase, I knew that I was about to strand myself up here in the mountains. Already the early afternoon light was beginning to fade. Fortunately I had ample fuel in the car, but on this narrow road it was impossible to turn the vehicle around.

Forced to go on, I approached a second village, a clutch of hovels built a century earlier around a now deconsecrated chapel. The only level place in which to turn a car was temporarily blocked by two peasants loading fire-wood onto a cart. As I waited for them to move away I realised how much poorer they were even than the people in the village below them. Their clothes were made partly from leather and partly from animal furs, and they carried shot-guns over their shoulders – weapons, I could tell from the way they looked at me, which they might not hesitate to use if I remained here after dark.

They watched me as I carefully reversed the car, their eyes roving across this expensive sports saloon, the camera equipment on the seat beside me, and even my clothes, all of which must have seemed unbelievably exotic.

To explain my presence, and give myself some kind of official status that would deter them from emptying their shot-guns into my back as I drove off, I said:

"I've been ordered to look for the aircraft – it came down somewhere near here."

I moved the gears, about to move off, when one of the men nodded in reply. He put one hand on my windshield, and with the other pointed to a narrow valley lying between twin mountain peaks a thousand feet above us.

As I drove up the mountain road, all my doubts had gone. This time, once and for all, I would prove my worth to a sceptical editor. Two separate witnesses had confirmed the presence of the crashed aircraft. Careful not to damage the car on this primitive track, I pressed on towards the valley high above me.

For the next two hours I moved steadily upwards, ever higher into these bleak mountains. By now all sight of the coastal plain and the sea had gone. Once I caught a brief glimpse of the first village I had passed, far below me like a small stain on a carpet. With luck, the road continued to carry me towards my goal. No more than an earth and stone track, it was barely wide enough to hold the car's wheels as I steered around the endless hairpin bends.

Twice more I stopped to question the few mountain people who watched me from the doors of their earth-floored hovels. However guardedly, they confirmed that the crashed aircraft lay above.

At four o'clock that afternoon, I finally reached the remote valley lying between two mountain peaks, and approached the last of the villages on this long trail. Here the road came to an end in a stony square surrounded by a cluster of dwellings. They looked as if they had been built 200 years earlier and had spent the intervening time trying to sink back into the mountain.

[91]

Most of the village was unpopulated, but to my surprise a few people came out of their houses to look at me, gazing with awe at the dusty car. Immediately I was struck by the extremity of their poverty. These people had nothing. They were destitute, not merely of worldly goods, but of religion, hope, and any knowledge of the rest of mankind. As I stepped from my car and lit a cigarette, waiting as they gathered around me at a respectful distance, it struck me as cruelly ironic that the huge airliner, the culmination of almost a century of aviation technology, should have come to its end here among these primitive mountain-dwellers.

Looking at their unintelligent and passive faces, I felt I was surrounded by a rare group of subnormals, a village of mental defectives amiable enough to be left on their own, high in this remote valley. Perhaps there was some mineral in the soil that damaged their nervous systems and kept them at this simple animal level.

"The aircraft – have you seen the airliner?" I called out. Some ten of the men and women were standing around me, mesmerised by the car, by my cigarette lighter and gold-rimmed glasses, even by my plump flesh.

"Aircraft – ? Here . . ." Simplifying my speech, I pointed to the rocky slopes and ravines above the village, but none of them seemed to understand me. Perhaps they were mute, or deaf. They were guileless enough, but it occurred to me that they might be concealing their knowledge of the crash. What riches they would reap from those thousand corpses, enough treasure to transform their lives for a century. I would have expected this small square to be piled high with aircraft seats, suitcases, bodies stacked like fire-wood.

"Aircraft . . ." Their leader, a small man with a sallow face no larger than my fist, repeated the word uncertainly. I realised immediately that none of them would know what I was talking about. Their dialect would be some remote sub-tongue, on the borders of intelligent speech.

Searching about for a way of reaching them, I noticed my airline bag packed with camera equipment. The identification tag carried a coloured picture of the huge airliner. Tearing it off the bag, I showed the picture around the group.

Immediately they were nodding away. They muttered to each

other, all pointing to a narrow ravine that formed a brief extension of the valley on the other side of the village. A cart track ran towards it, then faded into the stony soil.

"The airliner? It's up there? Good!" Delighted with them, I took out my wallet and showed them the large stack of bank-notes, my generous expenses for the film festival. Waving the notes encouragingly, I turned to the head-man. "You lead the way. We'll go there now. Many bodies, eh? Cadavers, everywhere?"

They were nodding together, eager eyes staring at the fan of bank-notes.

We set off in the car through the village, following the cart track along the hillside. Half a mile from the village we had to stop when the slope became too steep. The head-man pointed to the mouth of the ravine, and we climbed from the car and set off on foot. Still wearing my festival clothes, I found the going difficult. The floor of the gorge was covered with sharp stones that cut at my shoes. I fell behind my guide, who was scuttling over the stones like a goat.

It surprised me that there were still no signs of the giant airliner, of any debris or the hundreds of bodies. Looking around me, I expected the mountain to be drenched in corpses.

We had reached the end of the gorge. The final 300 feet of the mountain rose into the air towards the peak, separated from its twin by the valley and the village below. The head-man had stopped, and was pointing to the rocky wall. On his small face was a look of blunted pride.

"Where?" Catching my breath, I took the shroud off my camera lens. "There's nothing here."

Then I saw where he had guided me, and what the villagers all the way down to the coastal plain had described. Lying against the wall of the ravine were the remains of a three-engined military aircraft, its crushed nose and cockpit buried in the rocks. The fabric had long been stripped away by the wind, and the aircraft was little more than a collection of rusting spars and fuselage members. Obviously it had been here for more than thirty years, presiding like a tattered deity over this barren mountain. Somehow the fact of its presence had passed down the mountain from one village to the next.

The head-man pointed to the aircraft skeleton. He smiled at me, but his eyes were fixed on my chest, on the wallet in my breast pocket. Already his hand was slightly outstretched. For all his small size, he looked as dangerous as a wild dog.

I took out my wallet and handed him a single bank-note, worth more than he could earn in a month. Perhaps because the denomination was meaningless to him, he pointed aggressively at the other notes.

I fended him off. "Look – I'm not interested in this aircraft. It's the wrong one, you fool . . .!" When he stared uncomprehendingly at me I took the airline tag from my pocket and showed him the picture of the huge passenger jet. "This one! Very large. Hundreds of bodies." Losing my temper, and giving way completely to my outrage and disappointment, I screamed at him: "It's the wrong one! Can't you understand? There should be bodies everywhere, hundreds of cadavers . . .!"

He left me where I was, ranting away at the stony walls of this deserted ravine high in the mountains, and at the skeleton of this windblown reconnaissance plane.

Ten minutes later, when I returned to my car, I discovered that the slow puncture I had suspected earlier that afternoon had flattened one of the front tyres. Exhausted now, my shoes pierced by the rocks, my clothes filthy, I slumped behind the steering wheel, realising the futility of this absurd expedition. I would be lucky to make it back to the coast by night-fall. By then every other journalist would have reported the first sighting of the crashed airliner in the Pacific. My editor would be waiting with growing impatience for me to file my story in time for the evening newscasts. Instead, I was high in these barren mountains with a damaged car, my life possibly threatened by these idiot peasants.

After resting, I pulled myself together. It took me half an hour to change the wheel. As I started the engine and began the long drive back to the coastal plain the light had begun to fade even here at the peak.

The village was 300 yards below me when I could see the first of the hovels on a bend in the track. One of the villagers was standing beside a low wall, with what seemed to be a weapon in one hand. Immediately I slowed down, knowing that if they decided to attack me I had little hope of escape. I remembered the wallet in my pocket, and took it out, spreading the bank-notes on the seat. Perhaps I could buy my way through them.

As I approached, the man stepped forward into the road. The weapon in his hand was a crude spade. A small man, like all the others, his posture was in no way threatening. Rather, he seemed to be asking me for something, almost begging.

There was a bundle of old clothing on the verge beside the wall. Did he want me to buy it? As I slowed down, about to hand one of the bank-notes to him, I realised that it was an old woman, like a monkey wrapped in a shawl, staring sightlessly at me. Then I saw that her skull-like face was indeed a skull, and that the earth-stained rags were her shroud.

"Cadaver..." The man spoke nervously, fingering his spade in the dim light. I handed him the money and drove on, joining the road leading to the village.

Another younger man stood by the verge fifty yards ahead, also with a spade. The body of a small child, freshly disinterred, sat against the lid of its open coffin.

"Cadaver – "

All the way through the village people stood in the doorways, some alone, those who had no one to disinter for me, others with their spades. Freshly jerked from their graves, the corpses sat in the dim light in front of the hovels, propped against the stone walls like neglected relations, put out to at last earn their keep.

As I drove past, handing out the last of my money, I could hear the villagers murmuring, their voices following me down the mountainside.

(1975)

[95]

Report on an Unidentified Space Station

SURVEY REPORT 1

By good luck we have been able to make an emergency landing on this uninhabited space station. There have been no casualties. We all count ourselves fortunate to have found safe haven at a moment when the expedition was clearly set on disaster.

The station carries no identification markings and is too small to appear on our charts. Although of elderly construction it is soundly designed and in good working order, and seems to have been used in recent times as a transit depot for travellers resting at mid-point in their journeys. Its interior consists of a series of open passenger concourses, with comfortably equipped lounges and waiting rooms. As yet we have not been able to locate the bridge or control centre. We assume that the station was one of many satellite drogues surrounding a larger command unit, and was abandoned when a decline in traffic left it surplus to the needs of the parent transit system.

A curious feature of the station is its powerful gravitational field, far stronger than would be suggested by its small mass. However, this probably represents a faulty reading by our instruments. We hope shortly to complete our repairs and are grateful to have found shelter on this relic of the now forgotten migrations of the past.

Estimated diameter of the station: 500 metres.

SURVEY REPORT 2

Our repairs are taking longer than we first estimated. Certain pieces of equipment will have to be entirely rebuilt, and to shorten this task we are carrying out a search of our temporary home.

To our surprise we find that the station is far larger than we guessed. A thin local atmosphere surrounds the station, composed of interstellar dust attracted by its unusually high gravity. This fine vapour obscured the substantial bulk of the station and led us to assume that it was no more than a few hundred metres in diameter.

We began by setting out across the central passenger concourse that separates the two hemispheres of the station. This wide deck is furnished with thousands of tables and chairs. But on reaching the high partition doors 200 metres away we discovered that the restaurant deck is only a modest annexe to a far larger concourse. An immense roof three storeys high extends across an open expanse of lounges and promenades. We explored several of the imposing staircases, each equipped with a substantial mezzanine, and found that they lead to identical concourses above and below.

The space station has clearly been used as a vast transit facility, comfortably accommodating many thousands of passengers. There are no crew quarters or crowd control posts. The absence of even a single cabin indicates that this army of passengers spent only a brief time here before being moved on, and must have been remarkably self-disciplined or under powerful restraint.

Estimated diameter: 1 mile.

SURVEY REPORT 3

A period of growing confusion. Two of our number set out 48 hours ago to explore the lower decks of the station, and have so far failed to return. We have carried out an extensive search and fear that a tragic accident has taken place. None of the hundreds of elevators is in working order, but our companions may have entered an unanchored cabin and fallen to their deaths. We managed to force open one of the heavy doors and gazed with awe down the immense shaft. Many of the elevators within the station could comfortably carry a thousand passengers. We hurled several pieces of furniture down the shaft, hoping to time the interval before their impact, but not a sound returned to us. Our voices echoed away into a bottomless pit.

Perhaps our companions are marooned far from us on the lower levels? Given the likely size of the station, the hope remains that a maintenance staff occupies the crew quarters on some remote upper deck, unaware of our presence here.

Estimated diameter: 10 miles.

SURVEY REPORT 4

Once again our estimate of the station's size has been substantially revised. The station clearly has the dimensions of a large asteroid or even a small planet. Our instruments indicate that there are thousands of decks, each extending for miles across an undifferentiated terrain of passenger concourses, lounges and restaurant terraces. As before there is no sign of any crew or supervisory staff. Yet somehow a vast passenger complement was moved through this planetary waiting room.

While resting in the armchairs beneath the unvarying light we have all noticed how our sense of direction soon vanishes. Each of us sits at a point in space that at the same time seems to have no precise location but could be anywhere within these endless vistas of tables and armchairs. We can only assume that the passengers moving along these decks possessed some instinctive homing device, a mental model of the station that allowed them to make their way within it.

In order to establish the exact dimensions of the station and, if possible, rescue our companions we have decided to abandon our repair work and set out on an unlimited survey, however far this may take us.

Estimated diameter: 500 miles.

SURVEY REPORT 5

No trace of our companions. The silent interior spaces of the station have begun to affect our sense of time. We have been travelling in a straight line across one of the central decks for what seems an unaccountable period. The same pedestrian concourses, the same mezzanines attached to the stairways, and the same passenger lounges stretch for miles under an unchanging light. The energy needed to maintain this degree of illumination suggests that the operators of the station are used to a full passenger complement. However, there are unmistakable signs that no one has been here since the remote past.

We press on, following the same aisle that separates two adjacent lounge concourses. We rest briefly at fixed intervals, but despite our steady passage we sense that we are not moving at all, and may well be trapped within a small waiting room whose apparently infinite dimensions we circle like ants on a sphere. Paradoxically, our instruments confirm that we are penetrating a structure of rapidly increasing mass.

Is the entire universe no more than an infinitely vast space terminal?

Estimated diameter: 5000 miles.

Survey Report 6

We have just made a remarkable discovery! Our instruments have detected that a slight but perceptible curvature is built into the floors of the station. The ceilings recede behind us and dip fractionally towards the decks below, while the disappearing floors form a distinct horizon.

So the station is a curvilinear structure of finite form! There must be meridians that mark out its contours, and an equator that will return us to our original starting point. We all feel an immediate surge of hope. Already we may have stumbled on an equatorial line, and despite the huge length of our journey we may in fact be going home.

Estimated diameter: 50,000 miles.

Survey Report 7

Our hopes have proved to be short-lived. Excited by the thought that we had mastered the station, and cast a net around its invisible bulk, we were pressing on with renewed confidence. However, we now know that although these curvatures exist, they extend in all directions. Each of the walls curves away from its neighbours, the floors from the ceilings. The station, in fact, is an expanding structure whose size appears to increase exponentially. The longer the journey undertaken by a passenger, the greater the incremental distance he will have to travel. The virtually unlimited facilities of the station suggest that its passengers were embarked on extremely long, if not infinite journeys.

Needless to say, the complex architecture of the station has ominous implications for us. We realise that the size of the station is a measure, not of the number of passengers embarked – though this must have been vast – but of the length of the journeys undertaken within it. Indeed, there should ideally be only one passenger. A solitary voyager embarked on an infinite journey would require an infinity of transit lounges. As there are, fortunately, more than one of us we can assume that the station is a finite structure with the appearance of an infinite one. The degree to which it approaches an infinite size is merely a measure of the will and ambition of its passengers.

Estimated diameter: 1 million miles.

SURVEY REPORT 8

Just when our spirits were at their lowest ebb we have made a small but significant finding. We were moving across one of the limitless passenger decks, a prey to all fears and speculations, when we noticed the signs of recent habitation. A party of travellers has passed here in the recent past. The chairs in the central concourse have been disturbed, an elevator door has been forced, and there are the unmistakable traces left by weary voyagers. Without doubt there were more than two of them, so we must regretfully exclude our lost companions.

But there are others in the station, perhaps embarked on a journey as endless as our own!

We have also noticed slight variations in the decor of the station, in the design of light fittings and floor tiles. These may seem trivial, but multiplying them by the virtually infinite size of the station we

[100]

can envisage a gradual evolution in its architecture. Somewhere in the station there may well be populated enclaves, even entire cities, surrounded by empty passenger decks that stretch on forever like free space. Perhaps there are nation-states whose civilisations rose and declined as their peoples paused in their endless migrations across the station.

What force propelled them on their meaningless journeys? We can only hope that they were driven forward by the greatest of all instincts, the need to establish the station's size.

Estimated diameter: 5 light-years.

SURVEY REPORT 9

We are jubilant! A growing euphoria has come over us as we move across these great concourses. We have seen no further trace of our fellow passengers, and it now seems likely that we were following one of the inbuilt curvatures of the station and had crossed our own tracks.

But this small setback counts for nothing now. We have accepted the limitless size of the station, and this awareness fills us with feelings that are almost religious. Our instruments confirm what we have long suspected, that the empty space across which we travelled from our own solar system in fact lies within the interior of the station, one of the many vast lacunae set in its endlessly curving walls. Our solar system and its planets, the millions of other solar systems that constitute our galaxy, and the island universes themselves all lie within the boundaries of the station. The station is coeval with the cosmos, and constitutes the cosmos. Our duty is to travel across it on a journey whose departure point we have already begun to forget, and whose destination is the station itself, every floor and concourse within it.

So we move on, sustained by our faith in the station, aware that every step we take thereby allows us to reach a small part of that destination. By its existence the station sustains us, and gives our lives their only meaning. We are glad that in return we have begun to worship the station.

Estimated diameter: 15 million light-years.

(1982)

[101]

The Man Who Walked
on the Moon

I, too, was once an astronaut. As you see me sitting here, in this modest café with its distant glimpse of Copacabana Beach, you probably assume that I am a man of few achievements. The shabby briefcase between my worn heels, the stained suit with its frayed cuffs, the unsavoury hands ready to seize the first offer of a free drink, the whole air of failure . . . no doubt you think that I am a minor clerk who has missed promotion once too often, and that I amount to nothing, a person of no past and less future.

For many years I believed this myself. I had been abandoned by the authorities, who were glad to see me exiled to another continent, reduced to begging from the American tourists. I suffered from acute amnesia, and certain domestic problems with my wife and my mother. They now share my small apartment at Ipanema, while I am forced to live in a room above the projection booth of the Luxor Cinema, my thoughts drowned by the sound-tracks of science-fiction films.

So many tragic events leave me unsure of myself. Nonetheless, my confidence is returning, and a sense of my true history and worth. Chapters of my life are still hidden from me, and seem as jumbled as the film extracts which the projectionists screen each morning as they focus their cameras. I have still forgotten my years of training, and my mind bars from me any memory of the actual space-flights. But I am certain that I was once an astronaut.

*   *   *

Years ago, before I went into space, I followed many professions – freelance journalist, translator, on one occasion even a war correspondent sent to a small war, which unfortunately was never declared. I was in and out of newspaper offices all day, hoping for that one assignment that would match my talents.

Sadly, all this effort failed to get me to the top, and after ten years I found myself displaced by a younger generation. A certain reticence in my character, a sharpness of manner, set me off from my fellow journalists. Even the editors would laugh at me behind my back. I was given trivial assignments – film reviewing, or writing reports on office-equipment fairs. When the circulation wars began, in a doomed response to the onward sweep of television, the editors openly took exception to my waspish style. I became a part-time translator, and taught for an hour each day at a language school, but my income plummeted. My mother, whom I had supported for many years, was forced to leave her home and join my wife and myself in our apartment at Ipanema.

At first my wife resented this, but soon she and my mother teamed up against me. They became impatient with the hours I spent delaying my unhappy visits to the single newspaper office that still held out hope – my journey to work was a transit between one door slammed on my heels and another slammed in my face.

My last friend at the newspaper commiserated with me, as I stood forlornly in the lobby. "For heaven's sake, find a human-interest story! Something tender and affecting, that's what they want upstairs – life isn't an avant-garde movie!"

Pondering this sensible advice, I wandered into the crowded streets. I dreaded the thought of returning home without an assignment. The two women had taken to opening the apartment door together. They would stare at me accusingly, almost barring me from my own home.

Around me were the million faces of the city. People strode past, so occupied with their own lives that they almost pushed me from the pavement. A million human interest stories, of a banal and pointless kind, an encyclopaedia of mediocrity . . . Giving up, I left Copacabana Avenue and took refuge among the tables of a small café in a side-street.

It was there that I met the American astronaut, and began my own career in space.

The café terrace was almost deserted, as the office workers returned to their desks after lunch. Behind me, in the shade of the canvas awning, a fair-haired man in a threadbare tropical suit sat beside an empty glass. Guarding my coffee from the flies, I gazed at the small segment of sea visible beyond Copacabana Beach. Slowed by their mid-day meals, groups of American and European tourists strolled down from the hotels, waving away the jewellery salesmen and lottery touts. Perhaps I would visit Paris or New York, make a new life for myself as a literary critic . . .

A tartan shirt blocked my view of the sea and its narrow dream of escape. An elderly American, camera slung from his heavy neck, leaned across the table, his grey-haired wife in a loose floral dress beside him.

"Are you the astronaut?" the woman asked in a friendly but sly way, as if about to broach an indiscretion. "The hotel said you would be at this café . . ."

"An astronaut?"

"Yes, the astronaut Commander Scranton . . . ?"

"No, I regret that I'm not an astronaut." Then it occurred to me that this provincial couple, probably a dentist and his wife from the Corn Belt, might benefit from a well-informed courier. Perhaps they imagined that their cruise ship had berthed at Miami? I stood up, managing a gallant smile. "Of course, I'm a qualified translator. If you –"

"No, no . . ." Dismissing me with a wave, they moved through the empty tables. "We came to see Mr Scranton."

Baffled by this bizarre exchange, I watched them approach the man in the tropical suit. A nondescript fellow in his late forties, he had thinning blond hair and a strong-jawed American face from which all confidence had long been drained. He stared in a resigned way at his hands, which waited beside his empty glass, as if unable to explain to them that little refreshment would reach them that day. He was clearly undernourished, perhaps an ex-seaman who had jumped ship, one of thousands of down-and-outs trying to live by their wits on some of the hardest pavements in the world.

However, he looked up sharply enough as the elderly couple approached him. When they repeated their question about the astronaut he beckoned them to a seat. To my surprise, the waiter was summoned, and drinks were brought to the table. The husband unpacked his camera, while a relaxed conversation took place between his wife and this seedy figure.

"Dear, don't forget Mr Scranton . . ."

"Oh, please forgive me."

The husband removed several bank-notes from his wallet. His wife passed them across the table to Scranton, who then stood up. Photographs were taken, first of Scranton standing next to the smiling wife, then of the husband grinning broadly beside the gaunt American. The source of all this good humour eluded me, as it did Scranton, whose eyes stared gravely at the street with a degree of respect due to the surface of the moon. But already a second group of tourists had walked down from Copacabana Beach, and I heard more laughter when one called out: "There's the astronaut . . . !"

Quite mystified, I watched a further round of photographs being taken. The couples stood on either side of the American, grinning away as if he were a camel driver posing for pennies against a backdrop of the pyramids.

I ordered a small brandy from the waiter. He had ignored all this, pocketing his tips with a straight face.

"This fellow . . . ?" I asked. "Who is he? An astronaut?"

"Of course . . ." The waiter flicked a bottle-top into the air and treated the sky to a knowing sneer. "Who else but the man in the moon?"

The tourists had gone, strolling past the leatherware and jewellery stores. Alone now after his brief fame, the American sat among the empty glasses, counting the money he had collected.

The man in the moon?

Then I remembered the newspaper headline, and the exposé I had read two years earlier of this impoverished American who claimed to have been an astronaut, and told his story to the tourists for the price of a drink. At first almost everyone believed him, and he had become a popular figure in the hotel lobbies along Copacabana Beach. Apparently he had flown on one of the Apollo missions from Cape Kennedy in the 1970s, and his long-jawed face and stoical pilot's eyes seemed vaguely familiar from the magazine photographs. He was properly reticent, but if pressed with a tourist dollar could talk convincingly about the early lunar flights. In its way it was deeply moving to sit at a café table with a man who had walked on the moon . . .

Then an over-curious reporter exploded the whole pretence. No man named Scranton had ever flown in space, and the American authorities confirmed that his photograph was not that of any past or present astronaut. In fact he was a failed crop-duster from Florida who had lost his pilot's licence and whose knowledge of the Apollo flights had been mugged up from newspapers and television programmes.

Surprisingly, Scranton's career had not ended there and then, but moved on to a second tragi-comical phase. Far from consigning him to oblivion, the exposure brought him a genuine small celebrity. Banished from the grand hotels of Copacabana, he hung about the cheaper cafés in the side-streets, still claiming to have been an astronaut, ignoring those who derided him from their car windows. The dignified way in which he maintained his fraud tapped a certain good-humoured tolerance, much like the affection felt in the United States for those eccentric old men who falsely claimed to their deaths that they were veterans of the American Civil War.

So Scranton stayed on, willing to talk for a few dollars about his journey to the moon, quoting the same tired phrases that failed to convince the youngest schoolboy. Soon no one bothered to question him closely, and his chief function was to be photographed beside parties of visitors, an amusing oddity of the tourist trail.

But perhaps the American was more devious than he appeared, with his shabby suit and hangdog gaze? As I sat there, guarding the brandy I could barely afford, I resented Scranton's bogus celebrity, and the tourist revenue it brought him. For years I, too, had maintained a charade – the mask of good humour that I presented to my

[106]

colleagues in the newspaper world – but it had brought me nothing. Scranton at least was left alone for most of his time, something I craved more than any celebrity. When I compared our situations, there was plainly a strong element of injustice – the notorious British criminal who made a comfortable living being photographed by the tourists in the more expensive Copacabana restaurants had at least robbed one of Her Majesty's mail-trains.

At the same time, was this the human-interest story that would help me to remake my career? Could I provide a final ironic twist by revealing that, thanks to his exposure, the bogus astronaut was now doubly successful?

During the next days I visited the café promptly at noon. Notebook at the ready, I kept a careful watch for Scranton. He usually appeared in the early afternoon, as soon as the clerks and secretaries had finished their coffee. In that brief lull, when the shadows crossed from one side of the street to the other, Scranton would materialise, as if from a trapdoor in the pavement. He was always alone, walking straight-backed in his faded suit, but with the uncertainty of someone who suspects that he is keeping an appointment on the wrong day. He would slip into his place under the café awning, order a glass of beer from the sceptical waiter and then gaze across the street at the vistas of an invisible space.

It soon became clear that Scranton's celebrity was as threadbare as his shirt cuffs. Few tourists visited him, and often a whole afternoon passed without a single customer. Then the waiter would scrape the chairs around Scranton's table, trying to distract him from his reveries of an imaginary moon. Indeed, on the fourth day, within a few minutes of Scranton's arrival, the waiter slapped the table-top with his towel, already cancelling the afternoon's performance.

"Away, away . . . it's impossible!" He seized the newspaper that Scranton had found on a nearby chair. "No more stories about the moon . . ."

Scranton stood up, head bowed beneath the awning. He seemed resigned to this abuse. "All right . . . I can take my trade down the street."

To forestall this, I left my seat and moved through the empty tables.

"Mr Scranton? Perhaps we can speak? I'd like to buy you a drink."

"By all means." Scranton beckoned me to a chair. Ready for business, he sat upright, and with a conscious effort managed to bring the focus of his gaze from infinity to a distance of fifty feet away. He was poorly nourished, and his perfunctory shave revealed an almost tubercular pallor. Yet there was a certain resolute quality about this vagrant figure that I had not expected. Sitting beside him, I was aware of an intense and almost wilful isolation, not just in this foreign city, but in the world at large.

I showed him my card. "I'm writing a book of criticism on the science-fiction cinema. It would be interesting to hear your opinions. You are Commander Scranton, the Apollo astronaut?"

"That is correct."

"Good. I wondered how you viewed the science-fiction film . . . how convincing you found the presentation of outer space, the lunar surface and so on . . ."

Scranton stared bleakly at the table-top. A faint smile exposed his yellowing teeth, and I assumed that he had seen through my little ruse.

"I'll be happy to set you straight," he told me. "But I make a small charge."

"Of course." I searched in my pockets. "Your professional expertise, naturally . . ."

I placed some coins on the table, intending to hunt for a modest bank-note. Scranton selected three of the coins, enough to pay for a loaf of bread, and pushed the rest towards me.

"Science-fiction films – ? They're good. Very accurate. On the whole I'd say they do an excellent job."

"That's encouraging to hear. These Hollywood epics are not usually noted for their realism."

"Well . . . you have to understand that the Apollo teams brought back a lot of film footage."

"I'm sure." I tried to keep the amusement out of my voice. "The studios must have been grateful to you. After all, you could describe the actual moon-walks."

Scranton nodded sagely. "I acted as consultant to one of the

Hollywood majors. All in all, you can take it from me that those pictures are pretty realistic."

"Fascinating... coming from you that has authority. As a matter of interest, what was being on the moon literally like?"

For the first time Scranton seemed to notice me. Had he glimpsed some shared strain in our characters? This care-worn American had all the refinement of an unemployed car mechanic, and yet he seemed almost tempted to befriend me.

"Being on the moon?" His tired gaze inspected the narrow street of cheap jewellery stores, with its office messengers and lottery touts, the off-duty taxi-drivers leaning against their cars. "It was just like being here."

"So . . ." I put away my notebook. Any further subterfuge was unnecessary. I had treated our meeting as a joke, but Scranton was sincere, and anyway utterly indifferent to my opinion of him. The tourists and passing policemen, the middle-aged women sitting at a nearby table, together barely existed for him. They were no more than shadows on the screen of his mind, through which he could see the horizons of an almost planetary emptiness.

For the first time I was in the presence of someone who had nothing – even less than the beggars of Rio, for they at least were linked to the material world by their longings for it. Scranton embodied the absolute loneliness of the human being in space and time, a situation which in many ways I shared. Even the act of convincing himself that he was a former astronaut only emphasised his isolation.

"A remarkable story," I commented. "One can't help wondering if we were right to leave this planet. I'm reminded of the question posed by the Chilean painter Matta – 'Why must we fear a disaster in space in order to understand our own times?' It's a pity you didn't bring back any mementoes of your moon-walks."

Scranton's shoulders straightened. I could see him counting the coins on the table. "I do have certain materials . . ."

I nearly laughed. "What? A piece of lunar rock? Some moon dust?"

"Various photographic materials."

"Photographs?" Was it possible that Scranton had told the truth, and that he had indeed been an astronaut? If I could prove that the whole notion of his imposture was an error, an oversight by the journalist who had investigated the case, I would have the makings of a front-page scoop . . . "Could I see them? – perhaps I could use them in my book . . . ?"

"Well . . ." Scranton felt for the coins in his pocket. He looked hungry, and obviously thought only of spending them on a loaf of bread.

"Of course," I added, "I'll provide an extra fee. As for my book, the publishers might well pay many hundreds of dollars."

"Hundreds . . ." Scranton seemed impressed. He shook his head, as if amused by the ways of the world. I expected him to be shy of revealing where he lived, but he stood up and gestured me to finish my drink. "I'm staying a few minutes' walk from here."

He waited among the tables, staring across the street. Seeing the passers-by through his eyes, I was aware that they had begun to seem almost transparent, shadow players created by a frolic of the sun.

We soon arrived at Scranton's modest room behind the Luxor Cinema, a small theatre off Copacabana Avenue that had seen better days. Two former storerooms and an office above the projection booth had been let as apartments, which we reached after climbing a dank emergency stairway.

Exhausted by the effort, Scranton swayed against the door. He wiped the spit from his mouth onto the lapel of his jacket, and ushered me into the room. "Make yourself comfortable . . ."

A dusty light fell across the narrow bed, reflected in the cold-water tap of a greasy handbasin supported from the wall by its waste-pipe. Sheets of newspaper were wrapped around a pillow, stained with sweat and some unsavoury mucus, perhaps after an attack of malarial or tubercular fever.

Eager to leave this infectious den, I drew out my wallet. "The photographs . . . ?"

Scranton sat on the bed, staring at the yellowing wall behind me as if he had forgotten that I was there. Once again I was aware of his ability to isolate himself from the surrounding world, a talent I envied him, if little else.

"Sure . . . they're over here." He stood up and went to the suitcase that lay on a card table behind the door. Taking the money from me, he opened the lid and lifted out a bundle of magazines. Among them were loose pages torn from *Life* and *Newsweek*, and special supplements of the Rio newspapers devoted to the Apollo space-flights and the moon landings. The familiar images of Armstrong and the lunar module, the space-walks and splashdowns had been endlessly thumbed. The captions were marked with coloured pencil, as if Scranton had spent hours memorising these photographs brought back from the tideways of space.

I moved the magazines to one side, hoping to find some documentary evidence of Scranton's own involvement in the space-flights, perhaps a close-up photograph taken by a fellow astronaut.

"Is this it? There's nothing else?"

"That's it." Scranton gestured encouragingly. "They're good pictures. Pretty well what it was like."

"I suppose that's true. I had hoped . . ."

I peered at Scranton, expecting some small show of embarrassment. These faded pages, far from being the mementoes of a real astronaut, were obviously the prompt cards of an impostor. However, there was not the slightest doubt that Scranton was sincere.

I stood in the street below the portico of the Luxor Cinema, whose garish posters, advertising some science-fiction spectacular, seemed as inflamed as the mind of the American. Despite all that I had suspected, I felt an intense disappointment. I had deluded myself, thinking that Scranton would rescue my career. Now I was left with nothing but an empty notebook and the tram journey back to the crowded apartment in Ipanema. I dreaded the prospect of seeing my wife and my mother at the door, their eyes screwed to the same accusing focus.

Nonetheless, as I walked down Copacabana Avenue to the tram-stop, I felt a curious sense of release. The noisy pavements, the arrogant pickpockets plucking at my clothes, the traffic that aggravated the slightest tendency to migraines, all seemed to have receded, as if a small distance had opened between myself and the congested world. My meeting with Scranton, my brief involvement with this marooned man, allowed me to see everything in a more detached way. The businessmen with their briefcases, the afternoon tarts swinging their shiny handbags, the salesmen with their sheets of lottery tickets, almost deferred to me. Time and space had altered their perspectives, and the city was yielding to me. As I crossed the road to the tram-stop several minutes seemed to pass. But I was not run over.

This sense of a loosening air persisted as I rode back to Ipanema. My fellow passengers, who would usually have irritated me with their cheap scent and vulgar clothes, their look of bored animals in a menagerie, now scarcely intruded into my vision. I gazed down corridors of light that ran between them like the aisles of an open-air cathedral.

"You've found a story," my wife announced within a second of opening the door.

"They've commissioned an article," my mother confirmed. "I knew they would."

They stepped back and watched me as I made a leisurely tour of the cramped apartment. My changed demeanour clearly impressed them. They pestered me with questions, but even their presence was less bothersome. The universe, thanks to Scranton's example, had relaxed its grip. Sitting at the dinner table, I silenced them with a raised finger.

"I am about to embark on a new career . . ."

From then on I became ever more involved with Scranton. I had not intended to see the American again, but the germ of his loneliness had entered my blood. Within two days I returned to the café in the side-street, but the tables were deserted. I watched as two parties of tourists stopped to ask for "the astronaut". I then questioned the waiter, suspecting that he had banished the poor man. But, no, the American would be back the next day; he had been ill, or perhaps had secretly gone to the moon on business.

In fact, it was three days before Scranton at last appeared. Materialising from the afternoon heat, he entered the café and sat under the awning. At first he failed to notice that I was there, but Scranton's mere presence was enough to satisfy me. The crowds and traffic, which had begun once again to close around me, halted their clamour and withdrew. On the noisy street were imposed the silences of a lunar landscape.

However, it was all too clear that Scranton had been ill. His face was sallow with fever, and the effort of sitting in his chair soon tired him. When the first American tourists stopped at his table he barely rose from his seat, and while the photographs were taken he held tightly to the awning above his head.

By the next afternoon his fever had subsided, but he was so strained and ill-kempt that the waiter at first refused to admit him to the café. A trio of Californian spinsters who approached his table were clearly unsure that this decaying figure was indeed the bogus astronaut, and would have left had I not ushered them back to Scranton.

"Yes, this is Commander Scranton, the famous astronaut. I am his associate – do let me hold your camera . . ."

I waited impatiently for them to leave, and sat down at Scranton's table. Ill the American might be, but I needed him. After ordering a brandy, I helped Scranton to hold the glass. As I pressed the spinsters' bank-note into his pocket I could feel that his suit was soaked with sweat.

"I'll walk you back to your room. Don't thank me, it's in my direction."

"Well, I could use an arm." Scranton stared at the street, as if its few yards encompassed a Grand Canyon of space. "It's getting to be a long way."

"A long way! Scranton, I understand that . . ."

It took us half an hour to cover the few hundred yards to the Luxor Cinema. But already time was becoming an elastic dimension, and from then on most of my waking hours were spent with Scranton. Each morning I would visit the shabby room behind the cinema, bringing a paper bag of sweet-cakes and a flask of tea I had prepared in the apartment under my wife's suspicious gaze. Often the American had little idea who I was, but this no longer worried me. He lay in his narrow bed, letting me raise his head as I changed the sheets of newspaper that covered his pillow. When he spoke, his voice was too weak to be heard above the sound-tracks of the science-fiction films that boomed through the crumbling walls.

Even in this moribund state, Scranton's example was a powerful tonic, and when I left him in the evening I would walk the crowded streets without any fear. Sometimes my former colleagues called to me from the steps of the newspaper office, but I was barely aware of them, as if they were planetary visitors hailing me from the edge of a remote crater.

Looking back on these exhilarating days, I regret only that I never called a doctor to see Scranton. Frequently, though, the American would recover his strength, and after I had shaved him we would go down into the street. I relished these outings with Scranton. Arm in arm, we moved through the afternoon crowds, which seemed to part around us. Our fellow pedestrians had become remote and fleeting figures, little more than tricks of the sun. Sometimes, I could no longer see their faces. It was then that I observed the world through Scranton's eyes, and knew what it was to be an astronaut.

Needless to say, the rest of my life had collapsed at my feet. Having given up my work as a translator, I soon ran out of money, and was forced to borrow from my mother. At my wife's instigation, the features editor of the newspaper called me to his office, and made it plain that as an immense concession (in fact he had always been intrigued by my wife) he would let me review a science-fiction film at the Luxor. Before walking out, I told him that I was already too familiar with the film, and my one hope was to see it banned from the city forever.

So ended my connection with the newspaper. Soon after, the two women evicted me from my apartment. I was happy to leave them, taking with me only the reclining sun-chair on which my wife passed most of her days in preparation for her new career as a model. The sun-chair became my bed when I moved into Scranton's room.

By then the decline in Scranton's health forced me to be with him constantly. Far from being an object of charity, Scranton was now my only source of income. Our needs for several days could be met by a single session with the American tourists. I did my best to care for Scranton, but during his final illness I was too immersed in that sense of an emptying world even to notice the young doctor whose alarmed presence filled the tiny room. By a last irony, towards the end even Scranton himself seemed barely visible to me. As he died I was reading the mucus-stained headlines on his pillow.

After Scranton's death I remained in his room at the Luxor. Despite the fame he had once enjoyed, his burial at the Protestant cemetery was attended only by myself, but in a sense this was just, as he and I were the only real inhabitants of the city. Later I went through the few possessions in his suitcase, and found a faded pilot's log-book. Its pages confirmed that Scranton had worked as a pilot for a crop-spraying company in Florida throughout the years of the Apollo programme.

Nonetheless, Scranton had travelled in space. He had known the loneliness of separation from all other human beings, he had gazed at the empty perspectives that I myself had seen. Curiously, the pages torn from the news magazines seemed more real than the pilot's log-book. The photographs of Armstrong and his fellow astronauts were really of Scranton and myself as we walked together on the moon of this world.

I reflected on this as I sat at the small café in the side-street. As a gesture to Scranton's memory, I had chosen his chair below the awning. I thought of the planetary landscapes that Scranton had taught me to see, those empty vistas devoid of human beings. Already I was aware of a previous career, which my wife and the pressures of every-day life had hidden from me. There were the years of training for a great voyage, and a coastline similar to that of Cape Canaveral receding below me . . .

My reverie was interrupted by a pair of American tourists. A middle-aged man and his daughter, who held the family camera to her chin, approached the table.

"Excuse me," the man asked with an over-ready smile. "Are you the . . . the astronaut? We were told by the hotel that you might be here . . ."

I stared at them without rancour, treating them to a glimpse of

[115]

those eyes that had seen the void. I, too, had walked on the moon. "Please sit down," I told them casually. "Yes, I am the astronaut."

(1985)

The Enormous Space

I made my decision this morning – soon after eight o'clock, as I stood by the front door, ready to drive to the office. All in all, I'm certain that I had no other choice. Yet, given that this is the most important decision of my life, it seems strange that nothing has changed. I expected the walls to tremble, at the very least a subtle shift in the perspectives of these familiar rooms.

In a sense, the lack of any response reflects the tranquil air of this London suburb. If I were living, not in Croydon but in the Bronx or West Beirut, my action would be no more than sensible local camouflage. Here it runs counter to every social value, but is invisible to those it most offends.

Even now, three hours later, all is calm. The leafy avenue is as unruffled as ever. The mail has arrived, and sits unopened on the hall stand. From the dining-room window I watch the British Telecom engineer return to his van after repairing the Johnsons' telephone, an instrument reduced to a nervous wreck at least twice a month by their teenage daughters. Mrs Johnson, dressed in her turquoise track-suit, closes the gate and glances at my car. A faint vapour rises from the exhaust. The engine is still idling, all these hours after I began to demist the windscreen before finishing my breakfast.

This small slip may give the game away. Watching the car impatiently, I am tempted to step from the house and switch off the ignition, but I manage to control myself. Whatever happens, I must hold to my decision and all the consequences that flow from it. Fortunately, an Air India 747 ambles across the sky, searching none too strenuously for London Airport. Mrs Johnson, who shares something of its heavy-bodied elegance, gazes up at the droning turbo-fans. She is dreaming of Martinique or Mauritius, while I am dreaming of nothing.

My decision to dream that dream may have been made this morning, but I assume that its secret logic had begun to run through my life many months ago. Some unknown source of strength sustained me through the unhappy period of my car accident, convalescence and divorce, and the unending problems that faced me at the merchant bank on my return. Standing by the front door after finishing my coffee, I watched the mist clear from the Volvo's windscreen. The briefcase in my hand reminded me of the day-long meetings of the finance committee at which I would have to argue once again for the budget of my beleaguered research department.

Then, as I set the burglar alarm, I realised that I could change the course of my life by a single action. To shut out the world, and solve all my difficulties at a stroke, I had the simplest of weapons – my own front door. I needed only to close it, and decide never to leave my house again.

Of course, this decision involved more than becoming a mere stay-at-home. I remember walking into the kitchen, surprised by this sudden show of strength, and trying to work out the implications of what I had done. Still wearing my business suit and tie, I sat at the kitchen table, and tapped out my declaration of independence on the polished formica.

By closing the front door I intended to secede not only from the society around me. I was rejecting my friends and colleagues, my accountant, doctor and solicitor, and above all my ex-wife. I was breaking off all practical connections with the outside world. I would never again step through the front door. I would accept the air and the light, and the electric power and water that continued to flow through the meters. But otherwise I would depend on the outside world for nothing. I would eat only whatever food I could find within the house. After that I would rely on time and space to sustain me.

*   *   *

The Volvo's engine is still running. It is 3 p.m., seven hours after I first switched on the ignition, but I can't remember when I last filled the tank. It's remarkable how few passers-by have noticed the puttering exhaust – only the retired headmaster who patrols the avenue morning and afternoon actually stopped to stare at it. I watched him mutter to himself and shake his walking-stick before shuffling away.

The murmur of the engine unsettles me, like the persistent ringing of the telephone. I can guess who is calling: Brenda, my secretary; the head of marketing, Dr Barnes; the personnel manager, Mr Austen (I have already been on sick-leave for three weeks); the dental receptionist (a tender root canal reminds me that I had an appointment yesterday); my wife's solicitor, insisting that the first of the separation payments is due in six months' time.

Finally I pick up the telephone cable and pull the jack on this persistent din. Calming myself, I accept that I will admit to the house anyone with a legitimate right to be there – the TV rental man, the gas and electricity meter-readers, even the local police. I cannot expect to be left completely on my own. At the same time, it will be months before my action arouses any real suspicions, and I am confident that by then I will long since have moved into a different realm.

I feel tremendously buoyant, almost lightheaded. Nothing matters any more. Think only of essentials: the physics of the gyroscope, the flux of photons, the architecture of very large structures.

Five p.m. Time to take stock and work out the exact resources of this house in which I have lived for seven years.

First, I carry my unopened mail into the dining-room, open a box of matches and start a small, satisfying fire in the grate. To the flames I add the contents of my briefcase, all the bank-notes in my wallet, credit cards, driving licence and cheque-book.

I inspect the kitchen and pantry shelves. Before leaving, Margaret had stocked the freezer and refrigerator with a fortnight's supply of eggs, ham and other bachelor staples – a pointed gesture, bearing in mind that she was about to sail off into the blue with her lover (a tedious sales manager). These basic rations fulfil the same role as the keg of fresh water and sack of flour left at the feet of a marooned sailor, a reminder of the world rejecting him.

I weigh the few cartons of pasta in my hand, the jars of lentils and rice, the tomatoes and courgettes, the rope of garlic. Along with the tinned anchovies and several sachets of smoked salmon in the freezer, there are enough calories and protein to keep me going for at least ten days, three times that period if I ration myself. After that I will have to boil the cardboard boxes into a nutritious broth and rely on the charity of the wind.

At 6.15 the car's engine falters and stops.

In every way I am marooned, but a reductive Crusoe paring away exactly those elements of bourgeois life which the original Robinson so dutifully reconstituted. Crusoe wished to bring the Croydons of his own day to life again on his island. I want to expel them, and find in their place a far richer realm formed from the elements of light, time and space.

The first week has ended peacefully. All is well, and I have stabilised my regime most pleasantly. To my surprise, it has been remarkably easy to reject the world. Few people have bothered me. The postman has delivered several parcels, which I carry straight to the dining-room fireplace. On the third day my secretary, Brenda, called at the front door. I smiled winningly, reassured her that I was merely taking an extended sabbatical. She looked at me in her sweet but shrewd way – she had been strongly supportive during both my divorce and the crisis at the office – and then left with a promise to keep in touch. A succession of letters has arrived from Dr Barnes, but I warm my hands over them at the fireplace. The dining-room grate has become an efficient incinerator in which I have erased my entire past – passport; birth, degree and share certificates; uncashed traveller's cheques and 2000 French francs left from our last unhappy holiday in Nice; letters from my broker and orthopaedic surgeon. Documents of a dead past, they come to life briefly in the flame, and then write themselves into the dust.

Eliminating this detritus has kept me busy. I have pulled down the heavy curtains that hung beside the windows. Light has flooded into the rooms, turning every wall and ceiling into a vivid tabula rasa. Margaret had taken with her most of the ornaments and knick-knacks, and the rest I have heaved into a cupboard. Suffused with light, the house can breathe. Upstairs the windows are open to the sky. The rooms seem larger and less confined, as if they too have found freedom. I sleep well, and when I wake in the morning I almost feel myself on some Swiss mountain-top, with half the sky below me.

Without doubt, I am very much better. I have put away the past, a zone that I regret ever entering. I enjoy the special ease that comes from no longer depending on anyone else, however well-intentioned.

Above all, I am no longer dependent on myself. I feel no obligation to that person who fed and groomed me, who provided me with expensive clothes, who drove me about in his motor-car, who furnished my mind with intelligent books and exposed me to interesting films and art exhibitions. Wanting none of these, I owe that person, myself, no debts. I am free at last to think only of the essential elements of existence – the visual continuum around me, and the play of air and light. The house begins to resemble an advanced mathematical surface, a three-dimensional chessboard. The pieces have yet to be placed, but I feel them forming in my mind.

A policeman is approaching the house. A uniformed constable, he has stepped from a patrol car parked by the gate. He looks up at the roof, watched by an elderly couple who seem to have summoned him.

Confused, I debate whether to answer the doorbell. My arms and shirt are streaked with soot from the fireplace.

"Mr Ballantyne –?" A rather naïve young constable is looking me up and down. "Are you the householder?"

"Can I help you, officer?" I assume the convincing pose of a law-abiding suburbanite, interrupted in that act of lay worship, do-it-yourself.

"We've had reports of a break-in, sir. Your upstairs windows have been open all night – for two or three nights, your neighbours say. They thought you might be away."

"A break-in?" This throws me. "No, I've been here. In fact, I'm not planning to go out at all. I'm cleaning the chimneys, officer, getting rid of all that old soot and dust."

"Fair enough . . ." He hesitates before leaving, nose roving about for some irregularity he has sniffed, like a dog convinced of a hidden treat. He is certain that in some reprehensible way I am exploiting the suburban norms, like a wife-beater or child-molester.

I wait until he drives away, disappearing into that over-worked hologram called reality. Afterwards I lean against the door, exhausted by this false alarm. The effort of smiling at the officer reminds me of the interior distance I have travelled in the past week. But I must be careful, and hide behind those façades of conventional behaviour that I intend to subvert.

I close the windows that face the street, and then step with relief into the open bedrooms above the garden. The walls form sections of huge box-antennae tuned to the light. I think of the concrete inclines of the old racing track at Brooklands, and the giant chambers excavated from the bauxite cliffs at Les Baux, where Margaret first began to distance herself from me.

Of course a break-in has occurred, of a very special kind.

A month has passed, a period of many advances and a few setbacks. Resting in the kitchen beside the empty refrigerator, I eat the last of the anchovies and take stock of myself. I have embarked on a long internal migration, following a route partly inscribed within my head and partly within this house, which is a far more complex structure than I realised. I have a sense that there are more rooms than there appear to be at first sight. There is a richness of interior space of which I was totally unaware during the seven years I spent here with Margaret. Light floods everything, expanding the dimensions of walls and ceiling. These quiet streets were built on the site of the old Croydon aerodrome, and it is almost as if the perspectives of the former grass runways have returned to haunt these neat suburban lawns and the minds of those who tend them.

[122]

All this excitement has led me to neglect my rationing system. Scarcely anything is left in the pantry – a box of sugar cubes, a tube of tomato paste, and a few shrivelled asparagus tips. I lick my fingers and run them round the bottom of the empty bread bin. Already I find myself wishing that I had fully provisioned myself before embarking on this expedition. But everything I have achieved, the huge sense of freedom, of opened doors and of other doors yet to be opened, was contingent on my acting upon that decision of a moment.

Even so, I have to be careful not to give the game away. I maintain a reasonably kempt appearance, wave from the upstairs windows at Mrs Johnson and gesture apologetically at the overgrown lawn. She understands – I have been abandoned by my wife, condemned to the despair of a womanless world. I am hungry all the time, kept going by not much more than cups of sweetened tea. My weight has plunged; I have lost some fifteen pounds and feel permanently lightheaded.

Meanwhile, the outside world continues to bombard me with its irrelevant messages – junk mail, give-away newspapers, and a barrage of letters from Dr Barnes and the personnel department at the bank. They burn with heavy, solemn flames, and I assume that I have been sacked. Brenda called to see me three days ago, still puzzled by my cheerful demeanour. She told me that she had been reassigned, and that my office has been cleared of its files and furniture.

The letter-slot rattles. From the doormat I pick up two leaflets and a plastic envelope, a free sample of a new brand of chocolate. I rip it from the packing, and sink my teeth into the rubbery core, unable to control the saliva that swamps my mouth. I am so overwhelmed by the taste of food that I fail to hear the door-bell chiming. When I open the door I find a smartly-dressed woman in tweed suit and hat, presumably some solicitor's wife working as a volunteer almoner for the local hospital.

"Yes? Can I –?" With an effort I recognise her, as I lick the last of the chocolate from my teeth. "Margaret . . . ?"

"Of course." She shakes her head, as if this trivial social gaffe explains everything about me. "Who on earth did you think I was? Are you all right, Geoffrey?"

"Yes, I'm fine. I've been very busy. What are you looking for?" A frightening prospect crosses my mind. "You don't want to come back . . . ?"

"Good heavens, no. Dr Barnes telephoned me. He said that you'd resigned. I'm surprised."

"No, I decided to leave. I'm working on a private project. It's what I've always wanted to do."

"I know." Her eyes search the hall and kitchen, convinced that something has changed. "By the way, I've paid the electricity bill, but this is the last time."

"Fair enough. Well, I must get back to work."

"Good." She is clearly surprised by my self-sufficiency. "You've lost weight. It suits you."

The house relaxes its protective hold on me. When Margaret has gone I reflect on how quickly I have forgotten her. There are no tugs of old affection. I have changed, my senses tuned to all the wavelengths of the invisible. Margaret has remained in a more limited world, one of a huge cast of repertory players in that everlasting provincial melodrama called ordinary life.

Eager to erase her memory, I set off upstairs, and open the windows to enjoy the full play of afternoon sun. The west-facing rooms above the garden have become giant observatories. The dust cloaks everything with a mescalin haze of violet light, photons backing up as they strike the surface of window-sill and dressing-table. Margaret has taken many pieces of furniture with her, leaving unexpected gaps and intervals, as if this is a reversed spatial universe, the template of the one we occupied together. I can almost sit down in her absent William Morris chair, nearly see myself reflected in the missing art deco mirror whose chromium rim has left a shadow on the bathroom wall.

A curious discovery – the rooms *are* larger. At first I thought that this was an illusion brought about by the sparse furnishings, but the house has always been bigger than I realised. My eyes now see everything as it is, uncluttered by the paraphernalia of conventional life, as in those few precious moments when one returns from holiday and sees one's home in its true light.

Dazed by the vivid air, I blunder into Margaret's bedroom. The walls are strangely displaced, as if a team of scene-shifters have pulled them back to create a new stage set. There is no sign of the bed, and its bare mattress marked by the wine I spilled on the evening of her departure while commiserating over her dull lover. I have strayed into an unfamiliar area of the room, somewhere between Margaret's bathroom and the fitted cupboards. The remainder of the room sheers away from me, the walls pushed back by the light. For the first time I see the bed, but it seems as remote as an old divan at the rear of an empty warehouse.

Another door leads to a wide and silent corridor, clearly unentered for years. There is no staircase, but far away there are entrances to other rooms, filled with the sort of light that glows from X-ray viewing screens. Here and there an isolated chair sits against a wall, in one immense room there is nothing but a dressing-table, in another the gleaming cabinet of a grandfather clock presides over the endlessly carpeted floor.

The house is revealing itself to me in the most subtle way. Surprised by its perspectives, I trip over my own feet and feel my heart race ahead of me. I find a wall and press my hands to the striped paper, then fumble through the overlit air towards the landing. At last I reach the top of a huge staircase, whose banisters shrink together as I race to the safety of the floor below.

The true dimensions of this house may be exhilarating to perceive, but from now on I will sleep downstairs. Time and space are not necessarily on my side.

I have trapped a cat. So unnerved was I by the experience of losing myself in my own home that it takes me half an hour to realise that I have a small companion, Mrs Johnson's white Persian. While I was blundering around the Marienbad Palace that now occupies the first floor the cat entered the sitting-room through the open French window, and was trapped when a gust of air closed the door.

She follows me around amiably, waiting to be fed, but for once I am in need of her charity.

*   *   *

[125]

Two months have now passed. This conventional suburban villa is in fact the junction between our small illusory world and another larger and more real one. Miraculously, I have survived, though my last reserves of food were exhausted weeks ago. As I expected, Margaret paid a second and final visit. Still puzzled by my self-confidence and handsomely slimming figure, she told me that she would no longer be responsible for my mounting debts. I bade her farewell, and returned to my lunch of poodle pie.

The thought that I would never see Margaret again gave my modest meal an added relish, and afterwards I carefully set the dog-trap by the open door of the sitting-room. The untended garden with its knee-deep grass has attracted my neighbours' pets, trusting beasts who trundle happily towards me as I sit smiling in the arm-chair, cleaver concealed within an inviting cushion. By the time their ever-hopeful owners call round a few days later I have safely con-signed the bones to the space below the dining-room floorboards, a substantial ossuary that is the last resting-place of Bonzo, Major, Yorky and Mr Fred.

These dogs and cats, and the few birds I have been able to trap, soon formed my sole fare. However, it became clear that my neigh-bours were keeping a more careful eye on their pets, and I resigned myself to a diet of air. Fortunately, the television rental company intervened to provide a generous source of extra rations.

I remember the dour young man with the tool-kit who arrived to dismantle the attic aerial. He had made several earlier calls in the avenue, and had parked his van a hundred yards away. I followed him up the stairs, concerned that he too might lose his way among those vast rooms.

Sadly, my attempt to warn him came to nothing. As he stepped into the first of those white chambers, as large as aircraft hangars carved in the roof of an iceberg, he seemed to realise that he had entered a zone of danger. I grappled with him as we blundered through that white world, like Arctic explorers losing all sense of dis-tance within a few steps of their tent. An hour later, when I had calmed his fears and carried him down the staircase, he had sadly yielded to the terrors of light and space.

*   *   *

Three months – a period of continued discovery and few interruptions. The outside world has at last decided to leave me alone. I no longer answer the door, and there has been scarcely a caller, though threatening letters arrive from the local council, and from the water and electricity companies. But an unshakable logic is at work, and I am confident that my project will be complete before the power and water supplies are disconnected.

The house enlarges itself around me. The invasion of light which revealed its true dimensions has now reached the ground floor. To keep my bearings I have been forced to retreat into the kitchen, where I have moved my mattress and blankets. Now and then I venture into the hall and search the looming perspectives. It amazes me that Margaret and I once lived in this vast pile and so reduced it in our minds.

Already I can feel the walls of the kitchen distancing themselves from me. I spend all day here, sitting on the floor against the freezer cabinet. The cooker, refrigerator and dishwasher have become anonymous objects in some remote department store display. How much longer can this expansion continue? Sooner or later the process will halt, at that moment revealing the true dimensions of the world we inhabit, and which the visual centres of our timid brains have concealed from us. I am on the verge of a unique revelation, the equal perhaps of Columbus' discovery of the new world. I can scarcely wait to bring the news to my neighbours – the modest villa which Mrs Johnson imagines herself to occupy is in fact an immense Versailles!

Nearby, the bones of the TV repairman lie on the yellow linoleum like the ribs and skull of a long-decayed desert traveller.

Somewhere a door is being forced. I listen to the grating of keys testing a lock, then the sound of heels on the patio steps before a second attempt to prise open the French window.

Rousing myself, I sway across the kitchen, trying to steady my arms against the faraway washing-machine. A key turns, and a door opens somewhere beyond the great carpeted perspectives of the sitting-room.

A young woman has entered the house. As she returns the keys to her handbag I recognise Brenda, my former secretary. She stares at the dismantled dog-traps beside the window and then peers around the room, at last seeing me as I watch her beside the door.

"Mr Ballantyne? I'm sorry to break in. I was worried that you might..." She smiles reassuringly and takes the keys from her handbag. "Mrs Ballantyne said I could use the spare set. You haven't answered the phone, and we wondered if you'd fallen ill..."

She is walking towards me, but so slowly that the immense room seems to carry her away from me in its expanding dimensions. She approaches and recedes from me at the same time, and I am concerned that she will lose herself in the almost planetary vastness of this house.

Catching her as she swerves past me, I protect her from the outward rush of time and space.

I assume that we have entered the fourth month. I can no longer see the calendar on the kitchen door, so remote is it from me. I am sitting with my back to the freezer, which I have moved out of the kitchen into the pantry. But already the walls of this once tiny room constitute a universe of their own. The ceiling is so distant that clouds might form below it.

I have eaten nothing for the past week, but I no longer dare to leave the pantry and rarely venture more than a step from my position. I could easily lose my way crossing the kitchen and never be able to return to the only security and companionship that I know.

There is only one further retreat. So much space has receded from me that I must be close to the irreducible core where reality lies. This morning I gave in briefly to the sudden fear that all this has been taking place within my own head. By shutting out the world my mind may have drifted into a realm without yardsticks or sense of scale. For so many years I have longed for an empty world, and may unwittingly have constructed it within this house. Time and space have rushed in to fill the vacuum that I created. It even occurred to me to end the experiment, and I stood up and tried to reach the front door, a journey that seemed as doomed as Scott's return from the

[128]

South Pole. Needless to say, I was forced to give up the attempt long before crossing the threshold of the hall.

Behind me Brenda lies comfortably, her face only a few inches from my own. But now she too is beginning to move away from me. Covered by a jewelled frost, she rests quietly in the compartment of the freezer, a queen waiting one day to be reborn from her cryogenic sleep.

The perspective lines flow from me, enlarging the interior of the compartment. Soon I will lie beside her, in a palace of ice that will crystallise around us, finding at last the still centre of the world which came to claim me.

(1989)

Memories of the Space Age

I

All day this strange pilot had flown his antique aeroplane over the abandoned space centre, a frantic machine lost in the silence of Florida. The flapping engine of the old Curtiss biplane woke Dr Mallory soon after dawn, as he lay asleep beside his exhausted wife on the fifth floor of the empty hotel in Titusville. Dreams of the space age had filled the night, memories of white runways as calm as glaciers, now broken by this eccentric aircraft veering around like the fragment of a disturbed mind.

From his balcony Mallory watched the ancient biplane circle the rusty gantries of Cape Canaveral. The sunlight flared against the pilot's helmet, illuminating the cat's-cradle of silver wires that pinioned the open fuselage between the wings, a puzzle from which the pilot was trying to escape by a series of loops and rolls. Ignoring him, the plane flew back and forth above the forest canopy, its engine calling across the immense deserted decks, as if this ghost of the pioneer days of aviation could summon the sleeping titans of the Apollo programme from their graves beneath the cracked concrete.

Giving up for the moment, the Curtiss turned from the gantries and set course inland for Titusville. As it clattered over the hotel Mallory recognised the familiar hard brow behind the pilot's goggles. Each morning the same pilot appeared, flying a succession of antique craft – relics, Mallory assumed, from some forgotten museum at a private airfield nearby. There were a Spad and a Sopwith Camel, a replica of the Wright Flyer, and a Fokker triplane that had buzzed the NASA causeway the previous day, driving inland thousands of frantic gulls and swallows, denying them any share of the sky.

Standing naked on the balcony, Mallory let the amber air warm his skin. He counted the ribs below his shoulder blades, aware that for the first time he could feel his kidneys. Despite the hours spent foraging each day, and the canned food looted from the abandoned supermarkets, it was difficult to keep up his body weight. In the two months since they set out from Vancouver on the slow, nervous drive back to Florida, he and Anne had each lost more than thirty pounds, as if their bodies were carrying out a re-inventory of themselves for the coming world without time. But the bones endured. His skeleton seemed to grow stronger and heavier, preparing itself for the unnourished sleep of the grave.

Already sweating in the humid air, Mallory returned to the bedroom. Anne had woken, but lay motionless in the centre of the bed, strands of blond hair caught like a child's in her mouth. With its fixed and empty expression, her face resembled a clock that had just stopped. Mallory sat down and placed his hands on her diaphragm, gently respiring her. Every morning he feared that time would run out for Anne while she slept, leaving her forever in the middle of a last uneasy dream.

She stared at Mallory, as if surprised to wake in this shabby resort hotel with a man she had possibly known for years but for some reason failed to recognise.

"Hinton?"

"Not yet." Mallory steered the hair from her mouth. "Do I look like him now?"

"God, I'm going blind." Anne wiped her nose on the pillow. She raised her wrists, and stared at the two watches that formed a pair of time-cuffs. The stores in Florida were filled with abandoned clocks and watches, and each day Anne selected a new set of timepieces. She touched Mallory reassuringly. "All men look the same, Edward. That's streetwalker's wisdom for you. I meant the plane."

"I'm not sure. It wasn't a spotter aircraft. Clearly the police don't bother to come to Cape Canaveral any more."

"I don't blame them. It's an evil place. Edward, we ought to leave, let's get out this morning."

Mallory held her shoulders, trying to calm this frayed but still handsome woman. He needed her to look her best for Hinton. "Anne, we've only been here a week – let's give it a little more time."

"Time? Edward . . ." She took Mallory's hands in a sudden show of affection. "Dear, that's one thing we've run out of. I'm getting those headaches again, just like the ones I had fifteen years ago. It's uncanny, I can feel the same nerves . . ."

"I'll give you something, you can sleep this afternoon."

"No . . . They're a warning. I want to feel every twinge." She pressed the wristwatches to her temples, as if trying to tune her brain to their signal. "We were mad to come here, and even more mad to stay."

"I know. It's a long shot but worth a try. I've learned one thing in all these years – if there's a way out, we'll find it at Cape Canaveral."

"We won't! Everything's poisoned here. We should go to Australia, like all the other NASA people." Anne rooted in her handbag on the floor, heaving aside an illustrated encyclopaedia of birds she had found in a Titusville bookstore. "I looked it up – western Australia is as far from Florida as you can go. It's almost the exact antipodes. Edward, my sister lives in *Perth*. I knew there was a reason why she invited us there."

Mallory stared at the distant gantries of Cape Canaveral. It was difficult to believe that he had once worked there. "I don't think even Perth, Australia, is far enough. We need to set out into space again . . ."

Anne shuddered. "Edward, don't say that – a *crime* was committed here, everyone knows that's how it all began." As they listened to the distant drone of the aircraft she gazed at her broad hips and soft thighs. Equal to the challenge, her chin lifted. "Do you think Hinton is here? He may not remember me."

"He'll remember you. You were the only one who liked him."

"Well, in a sort of way. How long was he in prison before he escaped? Twenty years?"

"A long time. Perhaps he'll take you flying again. You enjoyed that."

"Yes . . . He was strange. But even if he is here, can he help? He was the one who started it all."

"No, not Hinton." Mallory listened to his voice in the empty hotel.

It seemed deeper and more resonant, as the slowing time stretched out the frequencies. "In point of fact, I started it all."

Anne had turned from him and lay on her side, a watch pressed to each ear. Mallory reminded himself to go out and begin his morning search for food. Food, a vitamin shot, and a clean pair of sheets. Sex with Anne, which he had hoped would keep them bickering and awake, had generated affection instead. Suppose they conceived a child, here at Cape Canaveral, within the shadow of the gantries . . . ?

He remembered the mongol and autistic children he had left behind in the clinic in Vancouver, and his firm belief – strongly contested by his fellow physicians and the worn-out parents – that these were diseases of time, malfunctions of the temporal sense that marooned these children on small islands of awareness, a few minutes in the case of the mongols, a span of micro-seconds for the autistics. A child conceived and born here at Cape Canaveral would be born into a world without time, an indefinite and unending present, that primeval paradise that the old brain remembered so vividly, seen both by those living for the first time and by those dying for the first time. It was curious that images of heaven or paradise always presented a static world, not the kinetic eternity one would expect, the roller-coaster of a hyperactive funfair, the screaming Luna Parks of LSD and psilocybin. It was a strange paradox that given eternity, an infinity of time, they chose to eliminate the very element offered in such abundance.

Still, if they stayed much longer at Cape Canaveral he and Anne would soon return to the world of the old brain, like those first tragic astronauts he had helped to put into space. During the previous year in Vancouver there had been too many attacks, those periods of largo when time seemed to slow, an afternoon at his desk stretched into days. His own lapses in concentration both he and his colleagues put down to eccentricity, but Anne's growing vagueness had been impossible to ignore, the first clear signs of the space sickness that began to slow the clock, as it had done first for the astronauts and then for all the other NASA personnel based in Florida. Within the last months the attacks had come five or six times a day, periods when everything began to slow down, and he would apparently spend all day shaving or signing a cheque.

Time, like a film reel running through a faulty projector, was moving at an erratic pace, at moments backing up and almost coming to a halt. One day it would stop, freeze forever on one frame. Had it really taken them two months to drive from Vancouver, weeks alone from Jacksonville to Cape Canaveral?

He thought of the long journey down the Florida coast, a world of immense empty hotels and glutinous time, of strange meetings with Anne in deserted corridors, of sex-acts that seemed to last for days. Now and then, in forgotten bedrooms, they came across other couples who had strayed into Florida, into the eternal present of this timeless zone, Paolo and Francesca forever embracing in the Fontainebleau Hotel. In some of those eyes there had been horror . . .

As for Anne and himself, time had run out of their marriage fifteen years ago, driven away by the spectres of the space complex, and by memories of Hinton. They had come back here like Adam and Eve returning to the Edenic paradise with an unfortunate dose of VD. Thankfully, as time evaporated, so did memory. He looked at his few possessions, now almost meaningless – the tape machine on which he recorded his steady decline; an album of nude Polaroid poses of a woman doctor he had known in Vancouver; his *Gray's Anatomy* from his student days, a unique work of fiction, pages still stained with formalin from the dissecting-room cadavers; a paperback selection of Muybridge's stop-frame photographs; and a psychoanalytic study of Simon Magus.

"Anne . . . ?" The light in the bedroom had become brighter, there was a curious glare, like the white runways of his dreams. Nothing moved, for a moment Mallory felt that they were waxworks in a museum tableau, or in a painting by Edward Hopper of a tired couple in a provincial bedroom. The dream-time was creeping up on him, about to enfold him. As always he felt no fear, his pulse was calmer . . .

There was a blare of noise outside, a shadow flashed across the balcony. The Curtiss biplane roared overhead, then sped low across the rooftops of Titusville. Roused by the sudden movement, Mallory stood up and shook himself, slapping his thighs to spur on his heart. The plane had caught him just in time.

"Anne, I think that was Hinton . . ."

She lay on her side, the watches to her ears. Mallory stroked her cheeks, but her eyes rolled away from him. She breathed peacefully with her upper lungs, her pulse as slow as a hibernating mammal's. He drew the sheet across her shoulders. She would wake in an hour's time, with a vivid memory of a single image, a rehearsal for those last seconds before time finally froze . . .

II

Medical case in hand, Mallory stepped into the street through the broken plate-glass window of the supermarket. The abandoned store had become his chief source of supplies. Tall palms split the sidewalks in front of the boarded-up shops and bars, providing a shaded promenade through the empty town. Several times he had been caught out in the open during an attack, but the palms had shielded his skin from the Florida sun. For reasons he had yet to understand, he liked to walk naked through the silent streets, watched by the orioles and parakeets. The naked doctor, physician to the birds . . . perhaps they would pay him in feathers, the midnight-blue tail-plumes of the macaws, the golden wings of the orioles, sufficient fees for him to build a flying machine of his own?

The medical case was heavy, loaded with packet rice, sugar, cartons of pasta. He would light a small fire on another balcony and cook up a starchy meal, carefully boiling the brackish water in the roof tank. Mallory paused in the hotel car-park, gathering his strength for the climb to the fifth floor, above the rat and cockroach line. He rested in the front seat of the police patrol car they had commandeered in a deserted suburb of Jacksonville. Anne had regretted leaving behind her classy Toyota, but the exchange had been sensible. Not only would the unexpected sight of this squad car confuse any military spotter planes, but the hotted-up Dodge could outrun most light aircraft.

Mallory was relying on the car's power to trap the mysterious pilot who appeared each morning in his antique aeroplanes. He had noticed that as every day passed these veteran machines tended to be of increasingly older vintage. Sooner or later the pilot would find himself well within Mallory's reach, unable to shake off the pursuing Dodge before being forced to land at his secret airfield.

Mallory listened to the police radio, the tuneless static that reflected the huge void that lay over Florida. By contrast the air-traffic frequencies were a babel of intercom chatter, both from the big jets landing at Mobile, Atlanta and Savannah, and from military craft overflying the Bahamas. All gave Florida a wide berth. To the north of the 31st parallel life in the United States went on as before, but south of that unfenced and rarely patrolled frontier was an immense silence of deserted marinas and shopping malls, abandoned citrus farms and retirement estates, silent ghettoes and airports.

Losing interest in Mallory, the birds were rising into the air. A dappled shadow crossed the car-park, and Mallory looked up as a graceful, slender-winged aircraft drifted lazily past the roof of the hotel. Its twin-bladed propeller struck the air like a child's paddle, driven at a leisurely pace by the pilot sitting astride the bicycle pedals within the transparent fuselage. A man-powered glider of advanced design, it soared silently above the rooftops, buoyed by the thermals rising from the empty town.

"Hinton!" Certain now that he could catch the former astronaut, Mallory abandoned his groceries and pulled himself behind the wheel of the police car. By the time he started the flooded engine he had lost sight of the glider. Its delicate wings, almost as long as an airliner's, had drifted across the forest canopy, kept company by the flocks of swallows and martins that rose to inspect this timorous intruder of their air-space. Mallory reversed out of the car-park and set off after the glider, veering in and out of the palms that lifted from the centre of the street.

Calming himself, he scanned the side roads, and caught sight of the machine circling the jai alai stadium on the southern outskirts of the town. A cloud of gulls surrounded the glider, some mobbing its lazy propeller, others taking up their station above its wing-tips. The pilot seemed to be urging them to follow him, enticing them with gentle rolls and yaws, drawing them back towards the sea and to the forest causeways of the space complex.

Reducing his speed, Mallory followed 300 yards behind the glider. They crossed the bridge over the Banana River, heading towards the NASA causeway and the derelict bars and motels of Cocoa Beach. The nearest of the gantries was still over a mile away to the north, but Mallory was aware that he had entered the outer zone of the space grounds. A threatening aura emanated from these ancient towers, as old in their way as the great temple columns of Karnak, bearers of a different cosmic order, symbols of a view of the universe that had been abandoned along with the state of Florida that had given them birth.

Looking down at the now clear waters of the Banana River, Mallory found himself avoiding the sombre forests that packed the causeways and concrete decks of the space complex, smothering the signs and fences, the camera towers and observation bunkers. Time was different here, as it had been at Alamagordo and Eniwetok; a psychic fissure had riven both time and space, then run deep into the minds of the people who worked here. Through that suture in his skull time leaked into the slack water below the car. The forest oaks were waiting for him to feed their roots, these motionless trees were as insane as anything in the visions of Max Ernst. There were the same insatiable birds, feeding on the vegetation that sprang from the corpses of trapped aircraft . . .

Above the causeway the gulls were wheeling in alarm, screaming against the sky. The powered glider side-slipped out of the air, circled and soared along the bridge, its miniature undercarriage only ten feet above the police car. The pilot pedalled rapidly, propeller flashing at the alarmed sun, and Mallory caught a glimpse of blond hair and a woman's face in the transparent cockpit. A red silk scarf flew from her throat.

"Hinton!" As Mallory shouted into the noisy air the pilot leaned from the cockpit and pointed to a slip road running through the forest towards Cocoa Beach, then banked behind the trees and vanished.

Hinton? For some bizarre reason the former astronaut was now masquerading as a woman in a blond wig, luring him back to the space complex. The birds had been in league with him . . .

The sky was empty, the gulls had vanished across the river into the

[137]

forest. Mallory stopped the car. He was about to step onto the road when he heard the drone of an aero-engine. The Fokker triplane had emerged from the space centre. It made a tight circuit of the gantries and came in across the sea. Fifty feet above the beach, it swept across the palmettos and saw-grass, its twin machine-guns pointing straight towards the police car.

Mallory began to re-start the engine, when the machine-guns above the pilot's windshield opened fire at him. He assumed that the pilot was shooting blank ammunition left over from some air display. Then the first bullets struck the metalled road a hundred feet ahead. The second burst threw the car onto its flattened front tyres, severed the door pillar by the passenger seat and filled the cabin with exploding glass. As the plane climbed steeply, about to make its second pass at him, Mallory brushed the blood-flecked glass from his chest and thighs. He leapt from the car and vaulted over the metal railings into the shallow culvert beside the bridge. His blood ran away through the water towards the waiting forest of the space grounds.

III

From the shelter of the culvert, Mallory watched the police car burning on the bridge. The column of oily smoke rose a thousand feet into the empty sky, a beacon visible for ten miles around the Cape. The flocks of gulls had vanished. The powered glider and its woman pilot – he remembered her warning him of the Fokker's approach – had slipped away to its lair somewhere south along the coast.

Too stunned to rest, Mallory stared at the mile-long causeway. It would take him half an hour to walk back to the mainland, an easy target for Hinton as he waited in the Fokker above the clouds. Had the former astronaut recognised Mallory and immediately guessed why the sometime NASA physician had come to search for him?

Too exhausted to swim the Banana River, Mallory waded ashore and set off through the trees. He decided to spend the afternoon in one of the abandoned motels in Cocoa Beach, then make his way back to Titusville after dark.

The forest floor was cool against his bare feet, but a soft light fell through the leafy canopy and warmed his skin. Already the blood had dried on his chest and shoulders, a vivid tracery like an aboriginal tattoo that seemed more suitable wear for this violent and uncertain realm than the clothes he had left behind at the hotel. He passed the rusting hulk of an Airstream trailer, its steel capsule overgrown with lianas and ground ivy, as if the trees had reached up to seize a passing space craft and dragged it down into the undergrowth. There were abandoned cars and the remains of camping equipment, moss-covered chairs and tables around old barbecue spits left here twenty years earlier when the sightseers had hurriedly vacated the state.

Mallory stepped through this terminal moraine, the elements of a forgotten theme park arranged by a demolition squad. Already he felt that he belonged to an older world within the forest, a realm of darkness, patience and unseen life. The beach was a hundred yards away, the Atlantic breakers washing the empty sand. A school of dolphins leapt cleanly through the water, on their way south to the Gulf. The birds had gone, but the fish were ready to take their place in the air.

Mallory welcomed them. He knew that he had been walking down this sand-bar for little more than half an hour, but at the same time he felt that he had been there for days, even possibly weeks and months. In part of his mind he had always been there. The minutes were beginning to stretch, urged on by this eventless universe free of birds and aircraft. His memory faltered, he was forgetting his past, the clinic at Vancouver and its wounded children, his wife asleep in the hotel at Titusville, even his own identity. A single moment was a small instalment of forever – he plucked a fern leaf and watched it for minutes as it fell slowly to the ground, deferring to gravity in the most elegant way.

Aware now that he was entering the dream-time, Mallory ran on through the trees. He was moving in slow motion, his weak legs carrying him across the leafy ground with the grace of an Olympic athlete. He raised his hand to touch a butterfly apparently asleep on the wing, embarking his outstretched fingers on an endless journey.

The forest that covered the sand-bar began to thin out, giving way to the beach-houses and motels of Cocoa Beach. A derelict hotel sat among the trees, its gates collapsed across the drive, Spanish moss hanging from a sign that advertised a zoo and theme park devoted to the space age. Through the waist-high palmettos the chromium and neon rockets rose from their stands like figures on amusement park carousels.

Laughing to himself, Mallory vaulted the gates and ran on past the rusting space ships. Behind the theme park were overgrown tennis courts, a swimming pool and the remains of the small zoo, with an alligator pit, mammal cages and an aviary. Happily, Mallory saw that the tenants had returned to their homes. An overweight zebra dozed in his concrete enclosure, a bored tiger stared in a cross-eyed way at his own nose, and an elderly caiman sunbathed on the grass beside the alligator pit.

Time was slowing now, coming almost to a halt. Mallory hung in mid-step, his bare feet in the air above the ground. Parked on the tiled path beside the swimming pool was a huge transparent dragonfly, the powered glider he had chased that morning.

Two wizened cheetahs sat in the shade under its wing, watching Mallory with their prim eyes. One of them rose from the ground and slowly launched itself towards him, but it was twenty feet away and Mallory knew that it would never reach him. Its threadbare coat, refashioned from some old carpet bag, stretched itself into a lazy arch that seemed to freeze forever in mid-frame.

Mallory waited for time to stop. The waves were no longer running towards the beach, and were frozen ruffs of icing sugar. Fish hung in the sky, the wise dolphins happy to be in their new realm, faces smiling in the sun. The water spraying from the fountain at the shallow end of the pool now formed a glass parasol.

Only the cheetah was moving, still able to outrun time. It was now ten feet from him, its head tilted to one side as it aimed at Mallory's throat, its yellow claws more pointed than Hinton's bullets. But Mallory felt no fear of this violent cat. Without time it could never reach him, without time the lion could at last lie down with the lamb, the eagle with the vole.

He looked up at the vivid light, noticing the figure of a young woman who hung in the air with outstretched arms above the diving board. Suspended over the water in a swallow dive, her naked body flew as serenely as the dolphins above the sea. Her calm face gazed at the glass floor ten feet below her small, extended palms. She seemed unaware of Mallory, her eyes fixed on the mystery of her own flight, and he could see clearly the red marks left on her shoulders by the harness straps of the glider, and the silver arrow of her appendix scar pointing to her childlike pubis.

The cheetah was drawing closer now, its claws picking at the threads of dried blood that laced Mallory's shoulders, its grey muzzle retracted to show its ulcerated gums and stained teeth. If he reached out he could embrace it, comfort all the memories of Africa, soothe the violence from its old pelt . . .

IV

Time had flowed out of Florida, as it had from the space age. After a brief pause, like a trapped film reel running free, it sped on again, rekindling a kinetic world.

Mallory sat in a deck chair beside the pool, watching the cheetahs as they rested in the shade under the glider. They crossed and uncrossed their paws like card-dealers palming an ace, now and then lifting their noses at the scent of this strange man and his blood.

Despite their sharp teeth, Mallory felt calm and rested, a sleeper waking from a complex but satisfying dream. He was glad to be surrounded by this little zoo with its backdrop of playful rockets, as innocent as an illustration from a children's book.

The young woman stood next to Mallory, keeping a concerned watch on him. She had dressed while Mallory recovered from his collision with the cheetah. After dragging away the boisterous beast she settled Mallory in the deck chair, then pulled on a patched leather flying suit. Was this the only clothing she had ever worn? A true child of the air, born and sleeping on the wing. With her over-bright mascara and blond hair brushed into a vivid peruke, she resembled a leather-garbed parakeet, a punk madonna of the airways. Worn NASA flashes on her shoulder gave her a biker's swagger. On the name-plate above her right breast was printed: *Nightingale.*

[141]

"Poor man – are you back? You're far, far away." Behind the child-like features, the soft mouth and boneless nose, a pair of adult eyes watched him warily. "Hey, you – what happened to your uniform? Are you in the police?"

Mallory took her hand, touching the heavy Apollo signet ring she wore on her wedding finger. From somewhere came the absurd notion that she was married to Hinton. Then he noticed her enlarged pupils, a hint of fever.

"Don't worry – I'm a doctor, Edward Mallory. I'm on holiday here with my wife."

"Holiday?" The girl shook her head, relieved but baffled. "That patrol car – I thought someone had stolen your uniform while you were . . . out. Dear doctor, no one comes on holiday to Florida any more. If you don't leave soon this is one vacation that may last forever."

"I know. . . ." Mallory looked round at the zoo with its dozing tiger, the gay fountain and cheerful rockets. This was the amiable world of the Douanier Rousseau's *Merry Jesters*. He accepted the jeans and shirt which the girl gave him. He had liked being naked, not from any exhibitionist urge, but because it suited the vanished realm he had just visited. The impassive tiger with his skin of fire belonged to that world of light. "Perhaps I've come to the right place, though – I'd like to spend forever here. To tell the truth, I've just had a small taste of what forever is going to be like."

"No, thanks." Intrigued by Mallory, the girl squatted on the grass beside him. "Tell me, how often are you getting the attacks?"

"Every day. Probably more than I realise. And you . . . ?" When she shook her head a little too quickly, Mallory added: "They're not that frightening, you know. In a way you want to go back."

"I can see. Take your wife and leave – any moment now all the clocks are going to stop."

"That's why we're here – it's our one chance. My wife has even less time left than I have. We want to come to terms with everything – whatever that means. Not much any more."

"Doctor . . . The real Cape Canaveral is inside your head, not out here." Clearly unsettled by the presence of this marooned physician, the girl pulled on her flying helmet. She scanned the sky, where the gulls and swallows were again gathering, drawn into the air by the distant drone of an aero-engine. "Listen – an hour ago you were nearly killed. I tried to warn you. Our local stunt pilot doesn't like the police."

"So I found out. I'm glad he didn't hit you. I thought he was flying your glider."

"Hinton? He wouldn't be seen dead in that. He needs speed. Hinton's trying to join the birds."

"Hinton . . ." Repeating the name, Mallory felt a surge of fear and relief, realising that he was committed now to the course of action he had planned months ago when he left the clinic in Vancouver. "So Hinton is here."

"He's here." The girl nodded at Mallory, still unsure that he was not a policeman. "Not many people remember Hinton."

"I remember Hinton." As she fingered the Apollo signet ring he asked: "You're not married to him?"

"To Hinton? Doctor, you have some strange ideas. What are your patients like?"

"I often wonder. But you know Hinton?"

"Who does? He has other things on his mind. He fixed the pool here, and brought me the glider from the museum at Orlando." She added, archly: "Disneyland East – that's what they called Cape Canaveral in the early days."

"I remember – twenty years ago I worked for NASA."

"So did my father." She spoke sharply, angered by the mention of the space agency. "He was the last astronaut – Alan Shepley – the only one who didn't come back. And the only one they didn't wait for."

"Shepley was *your* father?" Startled, Mallory turned to look at the distant gantries of the launching grounds. "He died in the Shuttle. Then you know that Hinton . . ."

"Doctor, I don't think it was Hinton who killed my father." Before Mallory could speak she lowered her goggles over her eyes. "Anyway, it doesn't matter now. The important thing is that someone will be here when he comes down."

"You're waiting for him?"

"Shouldn't I, doctor?"

"Yes . . . but it was a long time ago. Besides, it's a million to one against him coming down here."

"That's not true. According to Hinton, Dad may actually come down somewhere along this coast. Hinton says the orbits are starting to decay. I search the beaches every day."

Mallory smiled at her encouragingly, admiring this spunky but sad child. He remembered the news photographs of the astronaut's daughter, Gale Shepley, a babe in arms fiercely cradled by the widow outside the courtroom after the verdict. "I hope he comes. And your little zoo, Gale?"

"Nightingale," she corrected. "The zoo is for Dad. I want the world to be a special place for us when we go."

"You're leaving together?"

"In a sense – like you, doctor, and everyone else here."

"So you do get the attacks."

"Not often – that's why I keep moving. The birds are teaching me how to fly. Did you know that, doctor? The birds are trying to get out of time."

Already she was distracted by the unswept sky and the massing birds. After tying up the cheetahs she made her way quickly to the glider. "I have to leave, doctor. Can you ride a motorcycle? There's a Yamaha in the hotel lobby you can borrow."

But before taking off she confided to Mallory: "It's all wishful thinking, doctor, for Hinton, too. When Dad comes it won't matter any more."

Mallory tried to help her launch the glider, but the filmy craft took off within its own length. Pedalling swiftly, she propelled it into the air, climbing over the chromium rockets of the theme park. The glider circled the hotel, then levelled its long, tapering wings and set off for the empty beaches of the north.

Restless without her, the tiger began to wrestle with the truck tyre suspended from the ceiling of its cage. For a moment Mallory was tempted to unlock the door and join it. Avoiding the cheetahs chained to the diving board, he entered the empty hotel and took the staircase to the roof. From the ladder of the elevator house he watched the glider moving towards the space centre.

Alan Shepley – the first man to be murdered in space. All too well Mallory remembered the young pilot of the Shuttle, one of the last astronauts to be launched from Cape Canaveral before the curtain came down on the space age. A former Apollo pilot, Shepley had been a dedicated but likable young man, as ambitious as the other astronauts and yet curiously naïve.

Mallory, like everyone else, had much preferred him to the Shuttle's co-pilot, a research physicist who was then the token civilian among the astronauts. Mallory remembered how he had instinctively disliked Hinton on their first meeting at the medical centre. But from the start he had been fascinated by the man's awkwardness and irritability. In its closing days, the space programme had begun to attract people who were slightly unbalanced, and he recognised that Hinton belonged to this second generation of astronauts, mavericks with complex motives of their own, quite unlike the disciplined service pilots who had furnished the Mercury and Apollo flight-crews. Hinton had the intense and obsessive temperament of a Cortez, Pizarro or Drake, the hot blood and cold heart. It was Hinton who had exposed for the first time so many of the latent conundrums at the heart of the space programme, those psychological dimensions that had been ignored from its start and subsequently revealed, too late, in the crack-ups of the early astronauts, their slides into mysticism and melancholia.

"The best astronauts never dream," Russell Schweickart had once remarked. Not only did Hinton dream, he had torn the whole fabric of time and space, cracked the hour-glass from which time was running. Mallory was aware of his own complicity, he had been chiefly responsible for putting Shepley and Hinton together, guessing that the repressed and earnest Shepley might provide the trigger for a metaphysical experiment of a special sort.

At all events, Shepley's death had been the first murder in space, a crisis that Mallory had both stage-managed and unconsciously welcomed. The murder of the astronaut and the public unease that followed had marked the end of the space age, an awareness that man

[145]

had committed an evolutionary crime by travelling into space, that he was tampering with the elements of his own consciousness. The fracture of that fragile continuum erected by the human psyche through millions of years had soon shown itself, in the confused sense of time displayed by the inhabitants of the towns near the space centre. Cape Canaveral and the whole of Florida itself became a poisoned land to be forever avoided like the nuclear testing grounds of Nevada and Utah.

Yet, perhaps, instead of going mad in space, Hinton had been the first man to "go sane". During his trial he pleaded his innocence and then refused to defend himself, viewing the international media circus with a stoicism that at times seemed bizarre. That silence had unnerved everyone – how could Hinton believe himself innocent of a murder (he had locked Shepley into the docking module, vented his air supply and then cast him loose in his coffin, keeping up a matter-of-fact commentary the whole while) committed in full view of a thousand million television witnesses?

Alcatraz had been re-commissioned for Hinton, for this solitary prisoner isolated on the frigid island to prevent him contaminating the rest of the human race. After twenty years he was safely forgotten, and even the report of his escape was only briefly mentioned. He was presumed to have died, after crashing into the icy waters of the bay in a small aircraft he had secretly constructed. Mallory had travelled down to San Francisco to see the waterlogged craft, a curious ornithopter built from the yew trees that Hinton had been allowed to grow in the prison island's stony soil, boosted by a home-made rocket engine powered by a fertiliser-based explosive. He had waited twenty years for the slow-growing evergreens to be strong enough to form the wings that would carry him to freedom.

Then, only six months after Hinton's death, Mallory had been told by an old NASA colleague of the strange stunt pilot who had been seen flying his antique aircraft at Cape Canaveral, some native of the air who had so far eluded the half-hearted attempts to ground him. The descriptions of the bird-cage aeroplanes reminded Mallory of the drowned ornithopter dragged up onto the winter beach . . .

So Hinton had returned to Cape Canaveral. As Mallory set off on the Yamaha along the coast road, past the deserted motels and cocktail bars of Cocoa Beach, he looked out at the bright Atlantic sand, so unlike the rocky shingle of the prison island. But was the ornithopter a decoy, like all the antique aircraft that Hinton flew above the space centre, machines that concealed some other aim?

Some other escape?

V

Fifteen minutes later, as Mallory sped along the NASA causeway towards Titusville, he was overtaken by an old Wright biplane. Crossing the Banana River, he noticed that the noise of a second engine had drowned the Yamaha's. The venerable flying machine appeared above the trees, the familiar gaunt-faced pilot sitting in the open cockpit. Barely managing to pull ahead of the Yamaha, the pilot flew down to within ten feet of the road, gesturing to Mallory to stop, then cut back his engine and settled the craft onto the weed-grown concrete.

"Mallory, I've been looking for you! Come on, doctor!"

Mallory hesitated, the gritty backwash of the Wright's props stinging the open wounds under his shirt. As he peered among the struts Hinton seized his arm and lifted him onto the passenger seat.

"Mallory, yes . . . it's you still!" Hinton pushed his goggles back onto his bony forehead, revealing a pair of blood-flecked eyes. He gazed at Mallory with open amazement, as if surprised that Mallory had aged at all in the past twenty years, but delighted that he had somehow survived. "Nightingale just told me you were here. Doctor Mysterium . . . I nearly killed you!"

"You're trying again . . . !" Mallory clung to the frayed seat straps as Hinton opened the throttle. The biplane gazelled into the air. In a gust of wind across the exposed causeway it flew backwards for a few seconds, then climbed vertically and banked across the trees towards the distant gantries. Thousands of swallows and martins overtook them on all sides, ignoring Hinton as if well used to this erratic aviator and his absurd machines.

As Hinton worked the rudder tiller, Mallory glanced at this feverish and undernourished man. The years in prison and the rushing air

[147]

above Cape Canaveral had leached all trace of iron salts from his pallid skin. His raw eyelids, the nail-picked septum of his strong nose and his scarred lips were blanched almost silver in the wind. He had gone beyond exhaustion and malnutrition into a nervous realm where the rival elements of his warring mind were locked together like the cogs of an overwound clock. As he pummelled Mallory's arm it was clear that he had already forgotten the years since their last meeting. He pointed to the forest below them, to the viaducts, concrete decks and blockhouses, eager to show off his domain.

They had reached the heart of the space complex, where the gantries rose like gallows put out to rent. In the centre was the giant crawler, the last of the Shuttles mounted vertically on its launching platform. Its rusting tracks lay around it, the chains of an unshackled colossus.

Here at Cape Canaveral time had not stood still but moved into reverse. The huge fuel tank and auxiliary motors of the Shuttle resembled the domes and minarets of a replica Taj Mahal. Lines of antique aircraft were drawn up on the runway below the crawler – a Lilienthal glider lying on its side like an ornate fan window, a Mignet Flying Flea, the Fokker, Spad and Sopwith Camel, and a Wright Flyer that went back to the earliest days of aviation. As they circled the launch platform Mallory almost expected to see a crowd of Edwardian aviators thronging this display of ancient craft, pilots in gaiters and overcoats, women passengers in hats fitted with leather straps.

Other ghosts haunted the daylight at Cape Canaveral. When they landed Mallory stepped into the shadow of the launch platform, an iron cathedral shunned by the sky. An unsettling silence came in from the dense forest that filled the once open decks of the space centre, from the eyeless bunkers and rusting camera towers.

"Mallory, I'm glad you came!" Hinton pulled off his flying helmet, exposing a lumpy scalp under his close-cropped hair – Mallory remembered that he had once been attacked by a berserk warder. "I couldn't believe it was you! And Anne? Is she all right?"

"She's here, at the hotel in Titusville."

"I know, I've just seen her on the roof. She looked . . ." Hinton's voice dropped, in his concern he had forgotten what he was doing. He began to walk in a circle, and then rallied himself. "Still, it's good to see you. It's more than I hoped for – you were the one person who knew what was going on here."

"Did I?" Mallory searched for the sun, hidden behind the cold bulk of the launch platform. Cape Canaveral was even more sinister than he had expected, like some ancient death camp. "I don't think I –"

"Of course you knew! In a way we were collaborators – believe me, Mallory, we will be again. I've a lot to tell you . . ." Happy to see Mallory, but concerned for the shivering physician, Hinton embraced him with his restless hands. When Mallory flinched, trying to protect his shoulders, Hinton whistled and peered solicitously inside his shirt.

"Mallory, I'm sorry – that police car confused me. They'll be coming for me soon, we have to move fast. But you don't look too well, doctor. Time's running out, I suppose, it's difficult to understand at first . . ."

"I'm starting to. What about you, Hinton? I need to talk to you about everything. You look –"

Hinton grimaced. He slapped his hip, impatient with his undernourished body, an atrophied organ that he would soon discard. "I had to starve myself, the wingloading of that machine was so low. It took years, or they might have noticed. Those endless medical checks, they were terrified that I was brewing up an even more advanced psychosis – they couldn't grasp that I was opening the door to a new world." He gazed round at the space centre, at the empty wind. "We had to get out of time – that's what the space programme was all about . . ."

He beckoned Mallory towards a steel staircase that led up to the assembly deck six storeys above them. "We'll go topside. I'm living in the Shuttle – there's a crew module of the Mars platform still inside the hold, a damn sight more comfortable than most of the hotels in Florida." He added, with an ironic gleam: "I imagine it's the last place they'll come to look for me."

Mallory began to climb the staircase. He tried not to touch the greasy rivets and sweating rails, lowering his eyes from the tiled skin of the Shuttle as it emerged above the assembly deck. After all the years of thinking about Cape Canaveral he was still unprepared for the strangeness of this vast, reductive machine, a Juggernaut that could be pushed by its worshippers across the planet, devouring the years and hours and seconds.

Even Hinton seemed subdued, scanning the sky as if waiting for Shepley to appear. He was careful not to turn his back on Mallory, clearly suspecting that the former NASA physician had been sent to trap him.

"Flight and time, Mallory, they're bound together. The birds have always known that. To get out of time we first need to learn to fly. That's why I'm here. I'm teaching myself to fly, going back through all these old planes to the beginning. I want to fly without wings . . ."

As the Shuttle's delta wing fanned out above them, Mallory swayed against the rail. Exhausted by the climb, he tried to pump his lungs. The silence was too great, this stillness at the centre of the stopped clock of the world. He searched the breathless forest and runways for any sign of movement. He needed one of Hinton's machines to take off and go racketing across the sky.

"Mallory, you're going . . . ? Don't worry, I'll help you through it." Hinton had taken his elbow and steadied him on his feet. Mallory felt the light suddenly steepen, the intense white glare he had last seen as the cheetah sprang towards him. Time left the air, wavered briefly as he struggled to retain his hold on the passing seconds.

A flock of martins swept across the assembly deck, swirled like exploding soot around the Shuttle. Were they trying to warn him? Roused by the brief flurry, Mallory felt his eyes clear. He had been able to shake off the attack, but it would come again.

"Doctor – ? You'll be all right." Hinton was plainly disappointed as he watched Mallory steady himself at the rail. "Try not to fight it, doctor, everyone makes that mistake."

"It's going. . ." Mallory pushed him away. Hinton was too close to the rail, the man's manic gestures could jostle him over the edge. "The birds –"

"Of course, we'll join the birds! Mallory, we can all fly, every one of us. Think of it, doctor, true flight. We'll live forever in the air!"

"Hinton . . ." Mallory backed along the deck as Hinton seized the greasy rail, about to catapult himself onto the wind. He needed to get away from this madman and his lunatic schemes.

Hinton waved to the aircraft below, saluting the ghosts in their cockpits. "Lilienthal and the Wrights, Curtiss and Blériot, even old Mignet – they're here, doctor. That's why I came to Cape Kennedy. I needed to go back to the beginning, long before aviation sent us all off on the wrong track. When time stops, Mallory, we'll step from this deck and fly towards the sun. You and I, doctor, and Anne . . ."

Hinton's voice was deepening, a cavernous boom. The white flank of the Shuttle's hull was a lantern of translucent bone, casting a spectral light over the sombre forest. Mallory swayed forward, on some half-formed impulse he wanted Hinton to vault the rail, step out onto the air and challenge the birds. If he pressed his shoulders . . .

"Doctor – ?"

Mallory raised his hands, but he was unable to draw any nearer to Hinton. Like the cheetah, he was forever a few inches away.

Hinton had taken his arm in a comforting gesture, urging him towards the rail.

"Fly, doctor . . ."

Mallory stood at the edge. His skin had become part of the air, invaded by the light. He needed to shrug aside the huge encumbrance of time and space, this rusting deck and the clumsy tracked vehicle. He could hang free, suspended forever above the forest, master of time and light. He would fly . . .

A flurry of charged air struck his face. Fracture lines appeared in the wind around him. The transparent wings of a powered glider soared past, its propeller chopping at the sunlight.

Hinton's hands gripped his shoulders, bundling him impatiently over the rail. The glider slewed sideways, wheeled and flew towards them again. The sunlight lanced from its propeller, a stream of photons that drove time back into Mallory's eyes. Pulling himself free from Hinton, he fell to his knees as the young woman swept past in her glider. He saw her anxious face behind the goggles, and heard her voice shout warningly at Hinton.

But Hinton had already gone. His feet rang against the metal staircase. As he took off in the Fokker he called out angrily to Mallory, disappointed with him. Mallory knelt by the edge of the steel deck, waiting for time to flow back into his mind, hands gripping the oily rail with the strength of the new-born.

VI

TAPE 24: *17 August.*
Again, no sign of Hinton today.

Anne is asleep. An hour ago, when I returned from the drugstore, she looked at me with focused eyes for the first time in a week. By an effort I managed to feed her in the few minutes she was fully awake. Time has virtually stopped for her, there are long periods when she is clearly in an almost stationary world, a series of occasionally varying static tableaux. Then she wakes briefly and starts talking about Hinton and a flight to Miami she is going to make with him in his Cessna. Yet she seems refreshed by these journeys into the light, as if her mind is drawing nourishment from the very fact that no time is passing.

I feel the same, despite the infected wound on my shoulder – Hinton's dirty finger-nails. The attacks come a dozen times a day, everything slows to a barely perceptible flux. The intensity of light is growing, photons backing up all the way to the sun. As I left the drugstore I watched a parakeet cross the road over my head; it seemed to take two hours to fly fifty feet.

Perhaps Anne has another week before time stops for her. As for myself, three weeks? It's curious to think that at, say, precisely 3.47 p.m., 8 September, time will stop forever. A single micro-second will flash past unnoticed for everyone else, but for me will last an eternity. I'd better decide how I want to spend it!

TAPE 25: *19 August.*
A hectic two days. Anne had a relapse at noon yesterday, vaso-vagal

[152]

shock brought on by waking just as Hinton strafed the hotel in his Wright Flyer. I could barely detect her heartbeat, spent hours massaging her calves and thighs (I'd happily go out into eternity caressing my wife). I managed to stand her up, walked her up and down the balcony in the hope that the noise of Hinton's aircraft might jolt her back onto the rails. In fact, this morning she spoke to me in a completely lucid way, obviously appalled by my derelict appearance. For her it's one of those quiet afternoons three weeks ago.

We could still leave, start up one of the abandoned cars and reach the border at Jacksonville before the last minutes run out. I have to keep reminding myself why we came here in the first place. Running north will solve nothing. If there's a solution it's here, somewhere between Hinton's obsessions and Shepley's orbiting coffin, between the space centre and those bright, eerie transits that are all too visible at night. I hope I don't go out just as it arrives, spend the rest of eternity looking at the vaporising corpse of the man I helped to die in space. I keep thinking of that tiger. Somehow I can calm it.

TAPE 26: *25 August.*
3.30 p.m. The first uninterrupted hour of conscious time I've had in days. When I woke fifteen minutes ago Hinton had just finished strafing the hotel – the palms were shaking dust and insects all over the balcony. Clearly Hinton is trying to keep us awake, postponing the end until he's ready to play his last card, or perhaps until I'm out of the way and he's free to be with Anne.

I'm still thinking about his motives. He seems to have embraced the destruction of time, as if this whole malaise were an opportunity that we ought to seize, the next evolutionary step forward. He was steering me to the edge of the assembly deck, urging me to fly; if Gale Shepley hadn't appeared in her glider I would have dived over the rail. In a strange way he was helping me, guiding me into that new world without time. When he turned Shepley loose from the Shuttle he didn't think he was killing him, but setting him free.

The ever more primitive aircraft – Hinton's quest for a pure form of flight, which he will embark upon at the last moment. A Santos-Dumont flew over yesterday, an ungainly box-kite, he's given up his

World War I machines. He's deliberately flying badly designed aircraft, all part of his attempt to escape from winged aviation into absolute flight, poetical rather than aeronautical structures.

The roots of shamanism and levitation, and the erotic cathexis of flight – can one see them as an attempt to escape from time? The shaman's supposed ability to leave his physical form and fly with his spiritual body, the psychopomp guiding the souls of the deceased and able to achieve a mastery of fire, together seem to be linked with those defects of the vestibular apparatus brought on by prolonged exposure to zero gravity during the space flights. We should have welcomed them.

That tiger – I'm becoming obsessed with the notion that it's on fire.

TAPE 27: *28 August.*
An immense silence today, not a murmur over the soft green deck of Florida. Hinton may have killed himself. Perhaps all this flying is some kind of expiatory ritual, when he dies the shaman's curse will be lifted. But do I want to go back into time? By contrast, that static world of brilliant light pulls at the heart like a vision of Eden. If time *is* a primitive mental structure we're right to reject it. There's a sense in which not only the shaman's but all mystical and religious beliefs are an attempt to devise a world without time. Why did primitive man, who needed a brain only slightly larger than the tiger in Gale's zoo, in fact have a mind almost equal to those of Freud and Leonardo? Perhaps all that surplus neural capacity was there to release him from time, and it has taken the space age, and the sacrifice of the first astronaut, to achieve that single goal.

Kill Hinton . . . How, though?

TAPE 28: *3 September.*
Missing days. I'm barely aware of the flux of time any longer. Anne lies on the bed, wakes for a few minutes and makes a futile attempt to reach the roof, as if the sky offers some kind of escape. I've just brought her down from the staircase. It's too much of an effort to forage for food, on my way to the supermarket this morning the light was so bright that I had to close my eyes, hand-holding my way

around the streets like a blind beggar. I seemed to be standing on the floor of an immense furnace.

Anne is increasingly restless, murmuring to herself in some novel language, as if preparing for a journey. I recorded one of her drawn-out monologues, like some Gaelic love-poem, then speeded it up to normal time. An agonised "Hinton . . . Hinton . . ."

It's taken her twenty years to learn.

TAPE 29: *6 September.*
There can't be more than a few days left. The dream-time comes on a dozen stretches each day, everything slows to a halt. From the balcony I've just watched a flock of orioles cross the street. They seemed to take hours, their unmoving wings supporting them as they hung above the trees.

At last the birds have learned to fly.

Anne is awake . . .

(Anne): Who's learned to fly?

(EM): It's all right – the birds.

(Anne): Did you teach them? What am I talking about? How long have I been away?

(EM): Since dawn. Tell me what you were dreaming.

(Anne): Is this a dream? Help me up. God, it's dark in the street. There's no time left here. Edward, find Hinton. Do whatever he says.

VII

Kill Hinton . . .

As the engine of the Yamaha clacked into life, Mallory straddled the seat and looked back at the hotel. At any moment, as if seizing the last few minutes left to her, Anne would leave the bedroom and try to make her way to the roof. The stationary clocks in Titusville were about to tell the real time for her, eternity for this lost woman would be a flight of steps around an empty elevator shaft.

Kill Hinton . . . he had no idea how. He set off through the streets to the east of Titusville, shakily weaving in and out of the abandoned cars. With its stiff gearbox and unsteady throttle the Yamaha was exhausting to control. He was driving through an unfamiliar suburb of the town, a terrain of tract houses, shopping malls and car-parks laid out for the NASA employees in the building boom of the 1960s. He passed an overturned truck that had spilled its cargo of television sets across the road, and a laundry van that had careened through the window of a liquor store.

Three miles to the east were the gantries of the space centre. An aircraft hung in the air above them, a primitive helicopter with an overhead propeller. The tapering blades were stationary, as if Hinton had at last managed to dispense with wings.

Mallory pressed on towards the Cape, the engine of the motor-cycle at full throttle. The tracts of suburban housing unravelled before him, endlessly repeating themselves, the same shopping malls, bars and motels, the same stores and used-car lots that he and Anne had seen in their journey across the continent. He could almost believe that he was driving through Florida again, through the hundreds of small towns that merged together, a suburban universe in which these identical liquor stores, car-parks and shopping malls formed the building blocks of a strand of urban DNA generated by the nucleus of the space centre. He had driven down this road, across these silent intersections, not for minutes or hours but for years and decades. The unravelling strand covered the entire surface of the globe, and then swept out into space to pave the walls of the universe before it curved back on itself to land here at its departure point at the space centre. Again he passed the overturned truck beside its scattered television sets, again the laundry van in the liquor store window. He would forever pass them, forever cross the same intersection, see the same rusty sign above the same motel cabin . . .

"Doctor . . . !"

The smell of burning flesh quickened in Mallory's nose. His right calf was pressed against the exhaust manifold of the idling Yamaha. Charred fragments of his cotton trouser clung to the raw wound. As the young woman in the black flying suit ran across the street Mallory pushed himself away from the clumsy machine, stumbled over its spinning wheels and knelt in the road.

[156]

He had stopped at an intersection half a mile from the centre of Titusville. The vast planetary plain of parking lots had withdrawn, swirled down some cosmic funnel and then contracted to this small suburban enclave of a single derelict motel, two tract houses and a bar. Twenty feet away the blank screens of the television sets stared at him from the road beside the overturned truck. A few steps further along the sidewalk the laundry van lay in its liquor store window, dusty bottles of vodka and bourbon shaded by the wing-tip of the glider which Gale Shepley had landed in the street.

"Dr Mallory! Can you hear me? Dear man . . ." She pushed back Mallory's head and peered into his eyes, then switched off the still-clacking engine of the Yamaha. "I saw you sitting here, there was something . . . My God, your leg! Did Hinton . . . ?"

"No . . . I set fire to myself." Mallory climbed to his feet, an arm around the girl's shoulder. He was still trying to clear his head, there was something curiously beguiling about that vast suburban world . . . "I was a fool trying to ride it. I must see Hinton."

"Doctor, listen to me . . ." The girl shook his hands, her eyes wide with fever. Her mascara and hair were even more bizarre than he remembered. "You're dying! A day or two more, an hour maybe, you'll be gone. We'll find a car and I'll drive you north." With an effort she took her eyes from the sky. "I don't like to leave Dad, but you've got to get away from here, it's inside your head now."

Mallory tried to lift the heavy Yamaha. "Hinton – it's all that's left now. For Anne, too. Somehow I have to . . . kill him."

"He knows that, doctor – " She broke off at the sound of an approaching aero-engine. An aircraft was hovering over the nearby streets, its shadowy bulk visible through the palm leaves, the flicker of a rotor blade across the sun. As they crouched among the television sets it passed above their heads. An antique autogyro, it lumbered through the air like an aerial harvester, its free-spinning rotor apparently powered by the sunlight. Sitting in the open cockpit, the pilot was too busy with his controls to search the streets below.

Besides, as Mallory knew, Hinton had already found his quarry. Standing on the roof of the hotel, a dressing gown around her shoulders, was Anne Mallory. At last she had managed to climb the stairs, driven on by her dream of the sky. She stared sightlessly at the

[157]

autogyro, stepping back a single pace only when it circled the hotel and came in to land through a storm of leaves and dust. When it touched down on the roof the draught from its propellers stripped the gown from her shoulders. Naked, she turned to face the autogyro, lover of this strange machine come to save her from a time-reft world.

VIII

As they reached the NASA causeway huge columns of smoke were rising from the space centre. From the pillion seat of the motorcycle Mallory looked up at the billows boiling into the stained air. The forest was flushed with heat, the foliage glowing like furnace coals.

Had Hinton refuelled the Shuttle's engines and prepared the craft for lift-off? He would take Anne with him, and cast them both loose into space as he had done with Shepley, joining the dead astronaut in his orbital bier.

Smoke moved through the trees ahead of them, driven by the explosions coming from the launch site of the Shuttle. Gale throttled back the Yamaha and pointed to a break in the clouds. The Shuttle still sat on its platform, motors silent, the white hull reflecting the flash of explosions from the concrete runways.

Hinton had set fire to his antique planes. Thick with oily smoke, the flames lifted from the glowing shells slumped on their undercarts. The Curtiss biplane was burning briskly. A frantic blaze devoured the engine compartment of the Fokker, detonated the fuel tank and set off the machine-gun ammunition. The exploding cartridges kicked through the wings as they folded like a house of cards.

Gale steadied the Yamaha with her feet, and skirted the glowing trees 200 yards from the line of incandescent machines. The explosions flashed in her goggles, blanching her vivid make-up and giving her blond hair an ash-like whiteness. The heat flared against Mallory's sallow face as he searched the aircraft for any sign of Hinton. Fanned by the flames that roared from its fuselage, the autogyro's propeller rotated swiftly, caught fire and spun in a last blazing carnival. Beside it, flames raced along the wings of the

Wright Flyer; in a shower of sparks the burning craft lifted into the air and fell back upon the Sopwith Camel. Ignited by the intense heat, the primed engine of the Flying Flea roared into life, propelled the tiny aircraft in a scurrying arc among the burning wrecks, setting off the Spad and Blériot before it overturned in a furnace of rolling flame.

"Doctor – on the assembly deck!"

Mallory followed the girl's raised hand. A hundred feet above them, Anne and Hinton stood side by side on the metal landing of the stairway. The flames from the burning aircraft wavered against their faces, as if they were already moving through the air together. Although Hinton's hand was around Anne's waist, they seemed unaware of each other when they stepped forward into the light.

IX

As always during his last afternoons at Cocoa Beach, Mallory rested by the swimming pool of the abandoned hotel, watching the pale glider float patiently across the undisturbed skies of Cape Canaveral. In this peaceful arbour, surrounded by the drowsing inmates of the zoo, he listened to the fountain cast its crystal gems onto the grass beside his chair. The spray of water was now almost stationary, like the glider and the wind and the watching cheetahs, elements of an emblematic and glowing world.

As time slipped away from him, Mallory stood under the fountain, happy to see it transform itself into a glass tree that shed an opalescent fruit onto his shoulders and hands. Dolphins flew through the air over the nearby sea. Once he immersed himself in the pool, delighted to be embedded in this huge block of condensed time.

Fortunately, Gale Shepley had rescued him before he drowned. Mallory knew that she was becoming bored with him. She was intent now only on the search for her father, confident that he would soon be returning from the tideways of space. At night the trajectories were ever lower, tracks of charged particles that soared across the forest. She had almost ceased to eat, and Mallory was glad that once her father arrived she would at last give up her flying. Then the two of them would leave together.

Mallory had made his own preparations for departure. The key to the tiger cage he held always in his hand. There was little time left to him now, the light-filled world had transformed itself into a series of tableaux from a pageant that celebrated the founding days of creation. In the finale every element in the universe, however humble, would take its place on the stage in front of him.

He watched the tiger waiting for him at the bars of its cage. The great cats, like the reptiles before them, had always stood partly out of time. The flames that marked its pelt reminded him of the fire that had consumed the aircraft at the space centre, the fire through which Anne and Hinton still flew forever.

He left the pool and walked towards the tiger cage. He would unlock the door soon, embrace these flames, lie down with this beast in a world beyond time.

(1982)

Notes Towards
a Mental Breakdown

A[1] discharged[2] Broadmoor[3] patient[4] compiles[5] "Notes[6] Towards[7] a[8] Mental[9] Breakdown[10]", recalling[11] his[12] wife's[13] murder[14], his[15] trial[16] and[17] exoneration[18].

1

The use of the *indefinite* article encapsulates all the ambiguities that surround the undiscovered document, *Notes Towards a Mental Breakdown*, of which this 18-word synopsis is the only extant fragment. Deceptively candid and straightforward, the synopsis is clearly an important clue in our understanding of the events that led to the tragic death of Judith Loughlin in her hotel bedroom at Gatwick Airport. There is no doubt that the role of the still unidentified author was a central one. The self-effacing 'A' must be regarded not merely as an overt attempt at evasion but, on the unconscious level, as an early intimation of the author's desire to proclaim his guilt.

2

There is no evidence that the patient was discharged. Recent inspection of the in-patients' records at Springfield Hospital (cf. footnote 3) indicates that Dr Robert Loughlin has been in continuous detention in the Unit of Criminal Psychopathy since his committal at Kingston Crown Court on 18 May 1975. Only one visitor has called, a former colleague at the London Clinic, the neurologist Dr James Douglas, honorary secretary of the Royal College of Physicians Flying Club. It is possible that he may have given Dr Loughlin, with his obsessional interest in man-powered flight, the illusion that he had flown from the hospital on Douglas's back. Alternatively, "discharged" may be a screen memory of the revolver shot that wounded the Gatwick security guard.

3

Unconfirmed. Dr Loughlin had at no time in his ten-year career been either a patient or a member of the staff at Broadmoor Hospital. The reference to Broadmoor must therefore be taken as an indirect admission of the author's criminal motives or a confused plea of diminished responsibility on the grounds of temporary madness. Yet nothing suggests that Dr Loughlin considered himself either guilty of his wife's death or at any time insane. From the remaining documents – tape-recordings made in Suite B17 of the Inn on the Park Hotel (part of the floor occupied by the millionaire aviation pioneer Howard Hughes and his entourage during a visit to London) and cine-films taken of the runways at an abandoned USAAF base near Mildenhall – it is clear that Dr Loughlin believed he was taking part in a ritual of profound spiritual significance that would release his wife forever from the tragedy of her inoperable carcinoma. Indeed, the inspiration for this strange psychodrama may have come from the former Broadmoor laboratory technician and amateur dramatics coach, Leonora Carrington, whom Loughlin met at Elstree Flying Club, and with whom he had a brief but significant affair.

4

A remarkable feature of Dr Loughlin's confinement at Springfield is how little he conforms to the stereotype of "patient". Most of his fellow inmates at the Unit of Criminal Psychopathy are under some form of restraint, but Loughlin's behaviour is closer to that of a member of staff. He has informal access to all the facilities of the Unit, and with his medical training and powerful physique often stands in as an auxiliary nurse, even on occasion diagnosing minor ailments and supervising the administration of drugs. Characteristic of Loughlin is the high level of his general activity. He is forever moving about on errands, many of barely apparent significance, as if preparing for some important event in the future (or, conceivably, in the past). Much of his thought and energy is occupied by the construction of conceptual flying machines, using his bed, desk and personal cutlery. Recently, when his attempts to streamline all the furniture in the day-room unsettled the other patients, Dr Grumman encouraged Loughlin to write about his experiences as a weekend pilot. For the first time Loughlin was prepared to consider any aspect of his past, and immediately came up with a title, *Notes Towards a Mental Breakdown*.

5

What method Dr Loughlin employed in the preparation of this document has not been revealed, or indeed whether a single word exists other than the title. Given the powerful repressive forces at work, it seems likely that the author will employ any method other than that of straightforward narration. A clue may be found in Loughlin's previous experience as editor of the *Proceedings of the Institute of Neurosurgery*, and the habit of meticulous attention to editorial detail which he brought with him to Springfield. One manifestation of this obsession is his custom of annotating the books in the hospital library with copious footnotes. Several pages of the 1972 edition of *The British Pharmacopoeia Codex*, particularly those referring to anti-carcinogenetic drugs, have been so annotated that every word has been footnoted with imaginary aviation references.

6

Why Loughlin chose this term, with its suggestion of a preparatory sketch, to describe the most important and traumatic events of his life remains unclear. However, it is now known that this was not the only such document that he prepared. Two years earlier, during the first of his marital difficulties, Loughlin had kept a speculative diary, describing in minute detail the events of his personal and professional life. It seems that he was already aware of the erratic nature of his behaviour and of the recurrent fugues, each lasting several days, from which he would emerge in an increasingly dissociated state. At one point, after his wife's first nervous collapse, Loughlin secretly hired a private investigator to follow him, posing as her lover. Mr R. W. Butterworth of the Advance Detection Agency testified at Kingston Crown Court that he followed Loughlin and Leonora Carrington as they drove at random around eastern Suffolk, visiting one abandoned airfield after another. In his February 1975 Diaries (a few weeks before his wife's death) Loughlin describes his attempt to hire the main No. 2 runway at London Airport:

> "'Don't you understand, man, I only need it for half an hour. There's a special cargo going out.' Airport manager totally baffled. 'What, for heaven's sake?' But I couldn't tell him. I didn't know then."

7

Implicit in Loughlin's use of the preposition is the sense that he deliberately moved to meet his breakdown, constructing it of his own volition. This is confirmed by his behaviour in the months leading to his wife's death. Loughlin appears to have decided on a radically new course of action to save his wife, literally within the extreme metaphor of his own insanity. His wife's subsequent murder, his own breakdown and the entire period of his incarceration at Springfield must thus be regarded as a terminal metaphor, a labyrinth building itself from within which he began at last to unravel by writing *Notes Towards a Mental Breakdown*.

8

Again (cf. footnote 1) the use of the indefinite article underlines Loughlin's distance from his own crisis, which he now (January 1975) regarded as a complex of events and possibilities existing outside himself. Leaving his wife – who was bedridden in their Hendon apartment, cared for by Dr Douglas, her old friend and former lover – Loughlin embarked on a series of extended excursions around London and the Home Counties. Usually accompanied by Leonora Carrington, he visited the Mullard radio-observatory near Cambridge and the huge complex of early warning radar installations on the Suffolk coast. For some reason, empty swimming pools and multi-storey car-parks exerted a particular fascination. All these he seems to have approached as the constituents of 'a' mental breakdown which he might choose to recruit at a later date.

9

How far the events of this period (January to March 1975) were mentalised by Loughlin is hard to decide. To some extent all the factors surrounding Judith Loughlin's death – even the identity of her husband – may be said to be fictions of an over-worked imagination, as meaningless and as meaningful as the elaborate footnotes in *BP Codex*. Was Judith Loughlin suffering from cancer of the pancreas? What was the role of the young lexicographer and ice-dance champion, Richard Northrop, whom Loughlin treated at the London Clinic for migraine? The unmistakable elements of some kind of homo-erotic involvement hover in the background of their relationship. It may be that the apparent physical closeness of the two men masks the fact that they were one and the same man. Their holiday together, the three distressing weeks spent at the Gatwick hotel, and the shot fired at the airport security guard, inevitably recall Rimbaud and Verlaine, but Loughlin may well have passed the time there on his own waiting for his wife to appear with her lover, devising the identity of the lexicographer as a psychic "detonator". It is known that he spent much of his spare time stumbling around the airport ice rink.

10

A vital role seems to have been played during these last days by the series of paintings by Max Ernst entitled *Garden Airplane Traps*, pictures of low walls, like the brick-courses of an uncompleted maze, across which long wings have crashed, from whose joints visceral growths are blossoming. In the last entry of his diary, the day before his wife's death, 27 March 1975, Loughlin wrote with deceptive calm: "Ernst said it all in his comment on these paintings, the model for everything I've tried to do . . .

> *'Voracious gardens in turn devoured by a vegetation which springs from the debris of trapped airplanes . . . Everything is astonishing, heartbreaking and possible . . . with my eyes I see the nymph Echo . . .'* "

Shortly before writing out these lines he had returned to his Hendon apartment to find that his wife had set off for Gatwick Airport with Dr Douglas, intending to catch the 3.15 p.m. flight to Geneva the following day. After calling Richard Northrop, Loughlin drove straight to Elstree Flying Club.

11

The extent to which Loughlin retains any real "recall" of the events leading to his wife's death is doubtful. On occasions his memory is lucid and unbroken, but it soon becomes evident that he has re-mythologised the entire episode at Gatwick, as revealed in the following taped conversation between himself and Dr Grumman.

GRUMMAN: You say that you then drove to Elstree. Why?

LOUGHLIN: I had rented an aircraft there – a Piper Twin Comanche.

GRUMMAN: I see. Anyway, you then flew across London and on down to Gatwick, where you paralysed the airport for an hour by buzzing all the BEA jets parked on the ground.

LOUGHLIN: I knew that if I could find Judith's plane I could somehow fuse my aircraft with hers, in a kind of transfiguring . . .

GRUMMAN: . . . crash? But why?

LOUGHLIN: I was convinced that I could fly her to safety. It was the only way she would survive her cancer.

GRUMMAN: What actually happened?

LOUGHLIN: I landed and skidded into the nose-wheel of a VC10. Richard Northrop pulled me out. We had some sort of disagreement – he resented my dependence on him, and my involvement with Judith – and then the security guard was accidentally shot.

12

Although there is no doubt that Judith Loughlin had been married to her husband for three years, their relationship was never close, and she in no way could be regarded as "his". Before her marriage she had been involved in a long-standing liaison with Dr Douglas, whom she continued to see even after the latter's engagement and marriage in 1974. A successful barrister, self-willed and ambitious, she found herself increasingly unsympathetic towards Loughlin's erratic mental behaviour and incipient alcoholism. It is almost certain that but for her death she would have divorced Loughlin the following year. Viewing her charitably, one may say that her actions that fatal afternoon in the bathroom of her Gatwick hotel had been provoked by years of marital unhappiness.

13

Careful reconstruction of the events surrounding the murder of Judith Loughlin, on 28 March 1975, indicates that she had arrived at Gatwick with Dr Douglas the previous day. They passed the night in room 117 of the Skyport Hotel, intending to take the 3.15 p.m. flight to Geneva the following afternoon. It was while they were having lunch in the hotel restaurant that Loughlin appeared at the airport, already in an extreme state of alcoholic distress. He began a futile search among the parked airliners for the Trident jet then being prepared for the 3.15 flight, possibly intending to hijack the plane or even to blow it up with himself aboard. In the course of this search the security guard was shot. Loughlin then made his way to the Skyport Hotel, and by some ruse located and entered his wife's room. Befuddled by a heavy overdose of alcohol and amphetamines, he decided to revive himself in a bath of cold water. He was lying unconscious in the bath, fully clothed, when Judith Loughlin returned alone to her room after lunch.

14

All the evidence collected indicates that Judith Loughlin's decision to murder her husband was a sudden response to the sight of him slumped unconscious in her bath. Shocked by the damage he had done to the room – in his rage Loughlin had torn apart Dr Douglas's clothes and suitcases – she apparently decided to put an end to the sufferings of this unhappy man. Unfortunately she had reckoned neither with Loughlin's powerful physique – the moment she pressed his head below the bath water he leapt up and seized her – nor with the total transformation that had taken place within her husband's mind. Already he seems to have decided that she was leaving him only in the sense that she was dying of pancreatic cancer, and that he might save her by constructing a unique flying machine.

15

Questions as to the exact person indicated by this pronoun have been raised since the moment Loughlin was rescued from the fire blazing in room 117. It was first assumed from the ravings of the injured man that he was an airline pilot. He was sitting on the burning bed in the tandem position behind the charred body of a similarly seated woman, as if giving her pilot tuition. His wife had been forcibly trussed into a flying suit and wore helmet and goggles. She was identified by the double-helix of her intra-uterine device. Thanks to his sodden clothes, only Loughlin's hands and feet had been burned. The furniture in the room had been arranged to form a rough representation of an aircraft, perhaps inspired by the elaborate aeronautical motifs in the bedroom decor.

[168]

16

Not surprisingly, the trial exposed all the contradictions inherent in this puzzling case. Questions as to "Loughlin's" identity continued to be raised. There was no evidence that he was a qualified pilot, though a Private Pilot's Licence in his name was found in a locker at Elstree Flying Club, perhaps left there as part of a false identity carefully fabricated by him. Certainly he was obsessed with aviation, as his use of aircraft manufacturers' names for his medical colleagues indicates. Nor was there any real confirmation that he was a physician, particularly when we consider his lavish use of meaningless pseudo-medicalese (e.g. "serotonin[19] and[20] protein-reaction[21] suppressor[22] m.v.d.[23]" etc.).

17

This afterthought, attached to the previous 16 words with their apparently straightforward description of the events leading up to his trial, almost certainly indicates the author's real intent in compiling his ambiguous history.

18

The author's evident conviction of his own innocence, like his earlier belief that he had been discharged from hospital, may be taken as an expression of hope for the future. Meanwhile he continues with his busy round of activities in the Unit of Criminal Psychopathy, constructing his bizarre "aircraft" and tirelessly editing the footnotes with which he has annotated so many of the medical textbooks in the library. Ultimately the entire stock will have been provided with a unique gloss. As all these books are out-of-date, like the 1972 *BP Codex*, little harm is done. Most of his complex annotations have been shown to be complete fictions, an endlessly unravelling web of imaginary research work, medical personalities and the convoluted and sometimes tragic interrelationships of their private lives. Occasionally, however, they describe with unusual clarity a sequence of events that might almost have taken place. The patient seems trapped between what his psychiatrists call "paradoxical faces", each image of himself in the mirror reinforcing that in the glass behind him. The separation of the two will only be achieved by the appearance of the as yet incomplete document *Notes Towards a Mental Breakdown*, of which we possess only an 18-word synopsis and its set of footnotes. It seems possible that although the synopsis conceals a maze of lies and distortions, it is a simple and incontrovertible statement of the truth.

(1976)

The Index

Editor's note. From abundant internal evidence it seems clear that the text printed below is the index to the unpublished and perhaps suppressed autobiography of a man who may well have been one of the most remarkable figures of the 20th century. Yet of his existence nothing is publicly known, although his life and work appear to have exerted a profound influence on the events of the past fifty years. Physician and philosopher, man of action and patron of the arts, sometime claimant to the English throne and founder of a new religion, Henry Rhodes Hamilton was evidently the intimate of the greatest men and women of our age. After World War 2 he founded a new movement of spiritual regeneration, but private scandal and public concern at his growing megalomania, culminating in his proclamation of himself as a new divinity, seem to have led to his downfall. Incarcerated within an unspecified government institution, he presumably spent his last years writing his autobiography, of which this index is the only surviving fragment.

A substantial mystery still remains. Is it conceivable that all traces of his activities could be erased from our records of the period? Is the suppressed autobiography itself a disguised *roman à clef*, in which the fictional hero exposes the secret identities of his historical contemporaries? And what is the true role of the indexer himself, clearly a close friend of the writer, who first suggested that he embark on his autobiography? This ambiguous and shadowy figure has taken the unusual step of indexing himself into his own index. Perhaps the entire compilation is nothing more than a figment of the over-wrought imagination of some deranged lexicographer. Alternatively, the index may be wholly genuine, and the only glimpse we have into a world hidden from us by a gigantic conspiracy, of which Henry Rhodes Hamilton is the greatest victim.

A

Acapulco, 143

Acton, Harold, 142-7, 213

Alcazar, Siege of, 221-5

Alimony, HRH pays, 172, 247, 367, 453

Anaxagoras, 35, 67, 69-78, 481

Apollinaire, 98

Arden, Elizabeth, 189, 194, 376-84

Autobiography of Alice B. Toklas, The (Stein), 112

Avignon, birthplace of HRH, 9-13; childhood holidays, 27; research at Pasteur Institute of Ophthalmology, 101; attempts to restore anti-Papacy, 420-35

B

Bal Musette, Paris, 98

Balliol College, Oxford, 69-75, 231

Beach, Sylvia, 94-7

Berenson, Bernard, conversations with HRH, 134; offer of adoption, 145; loan of Dürer etching, 146; law-suits against HRH, 173-85

Bergman, Ingrid, 197, 234, 267

Biarritz, 123

Blixen, Karen von (Isak Dinesen), letters to HRH, declines marriage proposal, 197

Byron, Lord, 28, 76, 98, 543

C

Cambodia, HRH plans journey to, 188; crashes aircraft, 196; writes book about, 235; meetings with Malraux, 239; capture by insurgents, 253; escape, 261; writes second book about, 283

Cap d'Antibes, 218

Charing Cross Hospital Medical School, 78-93

Charterhouse, HRH enters, 31; academic distinction, 38; sexual crisis, 43; school captain, 44

Chiang Kai-shek, interviewed by HRH, 153; HRH and American arms embargo, 162; HRH pilots to Chungking, 176; implements land-reform proposals by HRH, 178; employs HRH as intermediary with Chou En-lai, 192

Churchill, Winston, conversations with HRH, 221; at Chequers with HRH, 235; spinal tap performed by HRH, 247; at Yalta with HRH, 298; 'iron curtain' speech, Fulton, Missouri, suggested by HRH, 312; attacks HRH in Commons debate, 367

Cocteau, Jean, 187

Cunard, Nancy, 204

D

D-Day, HRH ashore on Juno Beach, 223; decorated, 242

Dalai Lama, grants audience to HRH, 321; supports HRH's initiatives with Mao Tse-tung, 325; refuses to receive HRH, 381

Darwin, Charles, influence on HRH, 103; repudiated by HRH, 478

de Beauvoir, Simone, 176

de Gaulle, Charles, conversations with HRH, 319-47, 356-79, 401

Dealey Plaza (Dallas, Texas), rumoured presence of HRH, 435

Dietrich, Marlene, 234, 371, 435

E

Ecclesiastes, Book of, 87

Eckhart, Meister, 265

Einstein, Albert, first Princeton visit by HRH, 203; joint signatory with HRH and R. Niebuhr of Roosevelt petition, 276; second and third Princeton visits, 284; death-bed confession to HRH, 292